"Do people really live like this?"

"You city folks really do live in a bubble, don't you?" Kyle said.

"I'm sorry. I'm just...edgy," Ashlynn replied.

"It's no wonder you're edgy. I'm so sorry I got you into this."

"You didn't. Your fat

"But he—"

"Is not your fault."

"Still, I should never have let you...get close enough for him to notice."

"Stop it. You didn't even know he was out. Besides, I think it was me who started it."

He went very still. "Did you?"

And suddenly she couldn't continue the charade. Not with him. He was the most innocent person involved in all this, and yet he was the one who'd just uprooted his entire life to protect her. The very least she owed him was the truth.

"I know this is a cliché, but...we need to talk. Or rather I need to, and you need to listen."

"Is this going to include your real name?"

She drew in a deep breath. "Yes. And some other things."

"All right."

She gestured toward the big couch. "I think you'd better sit down."

Dear Reader,

I have to admit, when I saw that this Coltons series was mainly set in New York City, I hesitated. I've only been to the Big Apple once, and while it was an amazing experience, it was also a bit overwhelming. There's such a distinctive big-city East Coast vibe there, and it's not one I'm used to. Not one I was sure I could convey in the story, at least not believably. I'm a Westerner through and through.

But my editor, in all her wisdom, chose to give me the book set entirely in Montana, and that immediately changed my mind. Big Sky Country? Absolutely. Montana I could do. And that it was set on a ranch meant...horses! As a former horse owner and onetime wannabe barrel racer, I love putting them in my books. Especially when I can make them a genuine part of the story and the happy ending.

And a happy ending to a story involving a serial killer and a good man finding out some ugly truths may take some doing, but I think it also makes that ending all the more satisfying. I hope you feel the same way after your visit to Montana!

Happy reading,

Justine Davis

COLTON'S MONTANA HIDEAWAY

Justine Davis

Special thanks and acknowledgment are given to Justine Davis for her contribution to The Coltons of New York miniseries.

Recycling programs
for this product may
not exist in your area.

ISBN-13: 978-1-335-59378-8

Colton's Montana Hideaway

Copyright © 2023 by Harlequin Enterprises ULC

For questions and comments about the quality of this book, please contact us at CustomerService@Harlequin.com.

Harlequin Enterprises ULC
22 Adelaide St. West, 41st Floor
Toronto, Ontario M5H 4E3, Canada
www.Harlequin.com

Printed in U.S.A.

Justine Davis lives on Puget Sound in Washington State, watching big ships and the occasional submarine go by and sharing the neighborhood with assorted wildlife, including a pair of bald eagles, deer, a bear or two, and a tailless raccoon. In the few hours when she's not planning, plotting or writing her next book, her favorite things are photography, knitting her way through a huge yarn stash and driving her restored 1967 Corvette roadster—top down, of course.

Connect with Justine on her website, justinedavis.com, at Twitter.com/justine_d_davis or at Facebook.com/justinedaredavis.

Books by Justine Davis

Harlequin Romantic Suspense

The Coltons of New York

Colton's Montana Hideaway

Cutter's Code

Operation Homecoming
Operation Soldier Next Door
Operation Alpha
Operation Notorious
Operation Hero's Watch
Operation Second Chance
Operation Mountain Recovery
Operation Whistleblower
Operation Payback
Operation Witness Protection

The Coltons of Colorado

Colton's Dangerous Reunion

The Coltons of Grave Gulch

Colton K-9 Target

Visit the Author Profile page at Harlequin.com for more titles.

Chapter 1

Ashlynn Colton stared down at the hotel reservation confirmation on her new phone, both in a name not her own, questioning her own sanity. What on earth had she been thinking? She should have gone along with what her FBI agent brothers had wanted, should have gone into a safe house in familiar New York City, where people they trusted would look after her and protect her.

And you need looking after, if you're blind enough to get fooled so badly. So much for being the smartest one in any room.

If. That was the big question. They still didn't know for sure which of the six suspects they'd narrowed it down to was in fact the Landmark Killer, the twisted soul murdering innocent men simply because of their names and his fanatical devotion to another twisted soul, the imprisoned serial killer Maeve O'Leary.

But it couldn't be Xander. It just couldn't. Could it?

Her frequent casual lunch companion, with whom she'd had so many conversations about movies and music and this or that trend, and her own beloved tech, about which he was quite conversant? She just couldn't see it.

But she knew from her cousin, Sinead, an FBI profiler, that serial killers were very, very good at hiding who they were. And he was the only one with a discrepancy in two of his alibis. Discrepancies she herself had found. She, Ashlynn Colton, not the fictitious Zoe Lamont, the name on all that new ID she was carrying.

She lifted her gaze to the airplane's window, looking out at blue sky above and clouds below. Second-guessing wasn't in her nature, but she was learning fast now. She usually trusted her knowledge and her instincts. But this wasn't her usual realm of tech, of algorithms and search engines, this was not AI, this was reality, in its grimmest form.

And she was not an agent trained to deal with that kind of reality. She happily claimed the title of geek, and that did not include being able to defend herself either physically or with a gun. Her weapon, she always said, was her brain. She'd always been so proud to work at the FBI with her brothers, who were on everyone's list of the best agents at the Bureau.

Now she wasn't sure she even deserved the job she had.

And so you leave the city and the life you've known and head to the back of beyond, where you don't know anything?

Maybe she really had lost her mind. She'd certainly lost her grip, the moment she'd seen that text. That anonymous, untraceable text.

Your poor murdered daddy wouldn't be very proud of how little you've accomplished in HIS name. Should you even be alive yourself?

The Coltons had instantly become a united front, from her brothers to her cousin, Sinead. They knew who that text had come from, and they all insisted she needed to be in a safe house. She wasn't an agent, she didn't carry a gun and this was a determined serial killer. And suddenly, to her, even being in the same city with this twisted mind had seemed like too much. She needed time and space to think. To do what she did, search and research.

She'd also had a lead. A tiny one to be sure, one that would likely come to nothing, but it was enough to pursue. Well, maybe more of a link than a lead. At least it was something none of them had known about Xander. And tracking it down would get her out of the city into the bargain. She'd had to swear to be beyond careful, and remind them that she was an expert at both planting and burying things online as deep as they needed to go. Her careful work on constructed backgrounds had saved all of them at one time or another. They had finally given in, after securing her promise to stay safe and be untraceable.

But now, on board a jet headed to someplace she'd never been, in a part of the country she'd never been, she wasn't that certain of anything.

"Everything all right here, Ms. Lamont?"

There was that split-second delay while she realized the smiling flight attendant meant her. He was cute, in a mischievous kind of way that reminded her of her cousin Sinead's soon to be nephew, Harry. And somehow she didn't think the guy would mind being compared to a less-than-year-old baby. He was just too good-humored.

"As all right as it can be," she answered, smiling to take any complaint out of the words. The chaos she was dealing with was not his problem.

The thought of baby Harry brought to mind the apparent reconciliation between her brother Cash and his wife, Valentina. She'd always liked the woman; how could she not like someone with such a love of books and information that she'd become a librarian? And then there was her brother Brennan, who apparently was quite taken with, of all people, the reporter he'd suspected of selling him out not so long ago. Add in Sinead and her Sergeant Blackthorn, and that left only her brother Patrick unattached.

Well, and herself, of course, but she didn't count because she intended to keep her vow that she was done with the whole dating/falling in love thing. You can't lose a race you don't enter had become her motto.

Desperate for something to do that didn't involve making the same internet search with different parameters for a thirty-sixth time, she reached for the print magazine in the pocket on the back of the seat in front of her. She hadn't really held a print anything in her hands for so long it felt strange. Good, but strange. Even the photos looked different, glossier, in some ways prettier. She wondered how they got that effect on the luggage ad. If she had her computer out, she'd spend a bit of time figuring that out. But the bet with her brother Patrick, that she could go the entire flight without it, kept it secured in her backpack.

She turned the pages, hoping for something to read

that would occupy her ever spinning mind. She had another five hours to kill, and she was already twitchy. She'd flown out of LaGuardia because it had the only flights that made sense to her. No nonstop was bad enough, but flying due south to Florida only to board another plane and fly hours northwest, or to fly past her destination to Seattle and then turn around and fly back east made no sense to her logical mind. At least a plane change in Chicago or Denver was logical.

She paused at the next page turn, which had opened the magazine to a two-page spread featuring a panoramic aerial photograph. In the distance, but not too far, was a range of green-covered mountains topped by some puffy white clouds against a blue sky that seemed to go on forever.

Big Sky Country, isn't that their motto?

The foothills were a lighter green, leading down to a huge, flat valley. There was so much open space on the outer rim she felt uneasy just looking at it. She laughed inwardly at herself, but the sensation lingered. Maybe she should just stay at the hotel in the city where she'd reserved a room. But follow the evidence, isn't that what they always said? And ranch country was where the info she'd gathered pointed. How often had Xander told her of his hatred for the place he'd come from? There had to be a reason, something he'd left behind. And she would find it.

She looked back at the photo. In the foreground were several places she mentally connected to the state university she knew was there, a stadium and track and field setup, and a block or so away some sort of covered dome structure next to what she guessed might be a football field. Several buildings surrounded that area, likely the school itself, and maybe student housing?

Beyond that was what looked like small buildings in all directions, stretching out for maybe three or four miles, she thought, although it was only a guess. Lots of trees, lots of green; the picture must have been taken in spring or early summer. Maybe this was the suburbs of the city.

The puzzling part was the headline of the article indicating this was Bozeman, as if referring to the picture. The research she'd done said it was the fourth largest city in the state, but where was it? True, with a population of only fifty thousand–ish, it wouldn't be anything like what she was used to in New York, but…

She shifted to the caption of the photo. Read it twice to be sure. Flipped a page to the referenced information box. Stared at it for a moment.

The tallest building in the entire town was less than ten stories. Her New York born and bred mind couldn't wrap around it.

The photograph *was* Bozeman. All of it.

She should have done more research.

Chapter 2

Kyle Slater ran his hands over the long-legged, rangy young colt, who seemed to enjoy his touch. Unlike most others on the ranch, it seemed. Most of the hands complained about having to work with the sometimes recalcitrant horse, while Kyle asked for the chance. The animal had all the potential to be a standout, from his near-perfect conformation to his striking Appaloosa coloring. His black forequarters gleamed even in the stall's limited light, making the bright white splashed with black spots over his hindquarters stand out even more. The blanket with spots, as it was called, was classic, but a configuration like his was rare. With a white patch that seemed to flow down from just behind his withers to the top of his left front leg, plus white socks front and back and a near perfectly straight white blaze, he was beyond striking. He called the colt Splash, since he looked like a white horse someone had splashed black paint on, and his registered name was a long mouthful. His boss seemed okay with the name, had called it fitting and Kyle had even heard him using it when talking about the young horse.

"If it turns out you can throw that coat, Splash m' boy, you're going to have a happy life," he teased the animal now.

He stifled the imaginings that wanted to follow those words, his long-held dream of someday finding a young stud like this and breeding a line of quality horses. It was never going to happen. The closest he might get would be to work at a stud farm, and be part of somebody else's version of that dream coming true.

Splash nickered softly and nudged at his jacket pocket with his nose. "Looking for something? Oh, wait, it must be this," Kyle said, tugging out the three apple slices he'd secreted there.

The colt mouthed the pieces neatly and delicately off his palm. Kyle patted his neck before turning to go. The horse nickered again, this time sounding almost like a protest. Kyle looked back at the dark eyes fastened on him.

"I'll be back later," he promised as he left the stall.

He let out a long breath as he thought again that it wouldn't be long before he couldn't say that anymore. He'd be moving on, as he always did. He never spent more than a year in the same place or on the same job. He always moved on, never stayed. He hadn't for the last five years, ever since his life had blown up. And that year deadline was coming up soon.

He should be glad this time; working a dude ranch was hardly his idea of ranch work. No, give him a good, steady job at a working ranch, where all he had to do was deal with the animals, be they equine, bovine, or the occasional canine all day long.

There was too much people work here. He wasn't used to it and he didn't much like it. He didn't mind the kids so much; they were usually genuinely excited about being here. But the adults seemed to him to be either the type who would go back to their more civilized life and laugh about their week on a ranch and marvel that people actually lived that way, or those who were here reluctantly just to make their kids happy.

He liked those latter types a bit better, at least they were thinking of somebody other than themselves. Some even seemed like genuinely loving parents, not that he had any experience with that.

No, you've just got a murderer for a father, and it cost—

With the ease of long practice he derailed that train of thought before the painful memories could rise again. Not for the first time he thought of going farther, of leaving Montana altogether. He didn't like the idea; he loved this place where he'd been born. And there were plenty of places he hadn't worked yet.

He was going to miss that Appy colt, though. He'd like to see how he turned out, if he ended up half the horse Kyle suspected he could be. And if they didn't give up on the feisty animal and sell him.

He checked on the mare who'd suffered a nasty scrape when an arrogant teenager who thought she knew more than she did about riding had forced her down a rocky slope. She was healing well, would probably be fine by tomorrow, but hated being relegated to a stall in the meantime.

"I don't know how you put up with those dudes," he

told the docile animal as he made sure the wound was healing nicely, put on a fresh gauze pad and rewrapped it. "Tomorrow, sweetheart, you can probably be rid of that altogether."

She let out a lip-flapping sigh that made him smile. And she got the other half of the apple slices, which she took with delicate care.

"Slater! Five minutes!"

Matt Wesley's shout came from the doorway of the barn. The foreman—who also happened to be the son of the ranch's owner—was on top of things as usual, somehow managing to keep track of everyone who worked on the ranch, be they human or animal. No one could ever accuse the family of nepotism, because Matt was one of the best foremen he'd ever worked for, and there had been a few.

"I'll be there. Just finishing up on Daisy."

"Good," came the answer, and Kyle had no idea which part of his response it applied to. He knew the man was dedicated to the care of the horses, and that it was born out of more than just "they're the foundation of the business," as he often said. But he also knew Matt was well aware of Kyle's reluctance to deal with the dudes. Guests, he corrected himself, in keeping with what operations like this were calling them these days. So maybe he'd just been making sure Kyle wasn't going to bail on one of his least-liked tasks here at the Double W, that of teaching neophytes how to saddle up.

At least the ones who came to such sessions wanted to learn. A lot of the guests just wanted to mount up, ride, and when they were done hand off, as if the living, breathing, wonderful creature who was carrying

them was no more sentient than the car they handed off
to a valet.

City folks.

He gave Daisy a final pat and exited her stall, taking care to close and secure the bottom half of the door.
For all her docility, the mare was clever enough to take
advantage if he left her an opportunity.

He headed toward the barn door, wondering how
on earth he'd ever gotten himself into the position of
being, essentially, a teacher. He was lucky this wasn't
the high season at the ranch anymore, so there weren't
a lot of people coming through. Although when they
were busy he didn't have as much time to think, which
could be a positive, too.

When he reached Matt, the man stopped him. "Family," he said. "Watch the little boy, Dylan. They've had
a death. His big brother, and he's taking it hard."

Great. Well, at least he could relate. About the death,
not the brother. He had a half brother, or so the law
said, but if it was up to him he wouldn't claim the guy
any more than he'd claim the SOB that same law would
call his father. The man who'd slaughtered the first person he'd ever truly loved, and—despite his claims of
it being an accident—for no real reason other than she
made Kyle happy.

And Sarah had made him happy, for the first time
in his life. And probably the last time.

Hearing that either that brother or father was dead
would cause nothing more than a tiny ripple in his life,
and it would be a ripple of relief. So that wasn't going
to help. But if he thought of Sarah, of the horrendous
hole in his life and heart afterward, maybe he'd have a
clue about how this kid was feeling.

When he got out there, and saw the boy looking with interest at the flashy paint horse in the corral with the three other horses Hank Elliott—an older hand with a knack for matching horses and riders and a preference for going by just Elliott—had picked out for them, he thought there might be hope. Despite the shadows in eyes too young to look that haunted.

He'd try, anyway.

Even though this was the very reason he preferred to deal with animals.

With a three-and-a-half-hour layover in Denver, Ashlynn normally would have broken out her laptop and done…something. And she'd made the whole flight without it, as she'd promised Patrick she would. But although the custom-built device was as untraceable as she—and the FBI—could make it, she didn't trust a crowded place like an airport. It was too easy, even if you didn't use their public Wi-Fi, for someone, somehow to snake info, even if it was that woman over there who appeared to be making a video of the crowd but could just as easily be trying to capture keystrokes.

She tried for the distraction of looking once more at the unique airport that was Denver International. She gathered for the locals it was a love it or hate it situation, with nothing in between. She could see why. She understood the design with its white, tent-like peaks was meant to mimic the towering peaks of the Rocky Mountains in the distance, but she wasn't quite sure if that had been successful. But it was distinctive, in a one-of-a-kind way that made people stare. Whether that was good or bad she'd leave to the residents of Denver.

Her new burner phone, the team phone, buzzed an incoming message. She pulled it out with a sense of dread she'd never known before; she'd always been eager to see what any one of them had, hoping it would send her down a path that might lead to the resolution of a case. But now...

She unlocked the phone and tapped on the message notification.

He's gone quiet. No texts at all since the threat to Ashlynn. She found herself clenching her teeth as she tapped out an acknowledgment that she'd received the message.

She leaned back in the seat she'd taken, as close to the departure gate as she could manage. It was only an hour-and-forty-five-minute flight from here to Bozeman, and the ride she'd arranged should be waiting. She hoped the driver wasn't going to be the talkative sort. She was in no mood. Maybe she should have just taken the shuttle the hotel she'd chosen offered. Maybe the chatter of strangers would distract her.

When one of those strangers could be involved? What if he knew where she was going, what if he'd been tracking her, what if—

She cut the wild thoughts off. It was funny—well not funny, she wasn't laughing at all, but it was definitely disquieting—how different it was to be on the other side of a case. She spent her time doing what she loved, searching for clues, connections, pathways, all to lead to someone who needed to be stopped, put away, so people would no longer be in danger. But now she was the one in danger.

Should you even be alive yourself?

She suppressed a shiver. For the first time in her working life she had a real feeling for what her brothers faced in the field every day. Brennan and Cash especially, the twins both being special agents. Patrick perhaps a little less, being in the CSI unit which most often responded after the fact. But still…

The rational side of her brain told her it wasn't her job; her brothers told her the same, and not to worry about it. But she'd never been this close to it before, to the danger side of things.

She'd certainly never been personally threatened by a serial killer before.

Xander?

She still couldn't believe it. Maybe they were looking at it all wrong. Maybe the killer wasn't on the inside at all, maybe they were seeing intent where there was only coincidence. There could be an innocent explanation for everything. And the longer they went without stopping this murder spree, the more pressure—a lot of it from them themselves—there would be on them.

She sighed, pushing the thoughts aside. Felt a little jolt when a glance at the clock in the gate waiting area told her she'd been sitting there lost in that haze for well over an hour. She grimaced; if she were a field agent, she'd be long dead by now.

Even as the old gallows humor joke surfaced in her mind her current reality rendered it completely unfunny. Because she could easily be dead before this was over.

Chapter 3

Ashlynn finished her setup, made triply sure all her masking programs were operational, then went to the hotel room's mini fridge for a caffeine fix. They had her favorite soda, so she grabbed one gratefully, then walked back to the small desk. She was spoiled, used to having all the room she needed to spread out her notes, and multiple monitors, but she'd just have to make do. And this place had an advantage some didn't, a hard-wired network she could connect to, enabling her to use protocols to make herself even more untraceable.

She settled in to begin her search. Since she'd been the one who had spent time with Xander, she'd been assigned him to check out while the rest of the team pursued the other possible suspects. One of her first searches, running Xander's image through facial recognition had popped up one Victor Slater, of Elkton,

Montana, not far from where she now sat. And Victor apparently had another son, by another mother.

It was that tiny bit of information that had led her here to continue her search. That it could be completely wrong—she'd only found it by digging into Xander's background on the dark web, which wasn't her normal bailiwick—was something she was quite aware of. But when the team, aka her brothers, had ganged up on her and insisted she hide, coming here was the only thing that had popped into her head.

So here she was, in this place that was almost scary to her with its vaunted wide-open spaces and big sky, trying to do what would have been easier in her FBI office.

She ended up down a couple of rabbit holes; Slater was not that uncommon a name. And there was no surer way to end up at 3:00 a.m. knowing not much more regarding the case than she had before.

She decided she needed to take a chance and narrow things down a bit, so she tightened up her search parameters to five years either way from Xander's age. Between that and the connection with Xander's father's name and narrowing it down to western Montana as well, she got several hits, but only one that matched all three criteria.

Kyle Slater. Age twenty-seven. Born to Victor and Kyra Slater, of Elkton, MT.

She wrote down his date of birth. That he was the same age as she was barely registered as she plunged into the next task. She ran a check for a driver's license. The address that came back on the image was a ranch near Elkton, where he'd likely been working at the time it was issued.

The photo, as with many license photos, wasn't much help, it was rather grim faced and a tiny bit blurred, as if he'd moved just a fraction during the snap. The only thing she could be sure of was that as the physical description said, he did have red hair and brown eyes.

She tried for vehicles registered to him, and came up with a couple of the other Kyle Slaters she'd found, but nothing that seemed feasible, if her assumption he was still in the general area was correct. Of course she could well be wrong and this whole thing was the proverbial wild goose chase.

So she was down to the problem of confirming where he was now. She used every official database she had access to, but could find nothing except that there were multiple addresses attached to his name. The guy never seemed to spend much time in one place. She couldn't imagine living like that any more than her city-bred mind could wrap around living somewhere like this in the first place, without a skyscraper in sight.

She looked closer at the location data and it appeared he changed locations every year. Or at least he had starting five years ago. And the last address change had been six months ago. So if he stayed true to habit, he should still be wherever he'd ended up this last move. But there was no data yet on the new location.

She looked at the list of locations she'd made again.

Four places.

All in western Montana.

All ranches.

So he was what, a cowboy or something? They did still exist, didn't they? Somebody had to take care of the cows on ranches, right? And surely they had to make enough money to file taxes?

She dug deeper. Tax returns. There it was, ranch hand. Wow, they didn't make much. But she supposed they lived on the ranch, in some sort of bunkhouse or something, so that would lower their cost of living. Or was she imagining things based on the old Westerns her mother used to watch after Dad was killed, saying she wished for a simpler time?

But until he filed a new return, there was no way of knowing where he was now. And by then the Landmark Killer could have worked his way through to the *Y* in Maeve O'Leary's name.

She stared at the helpful but not complete data on her screen, going from window to window. Weary of it, she leaned back in the chair that clearly wasn't designed for the hours she spent like this. She pondered the fact that she was hungry, and picked up the room service menu; she wouldn't leave her system vulnerable, and it was too much work to take it all down then set up again, just to go out and eat somewhere.

She scanned the items, smiling at some of the things you would never see in New York City. A bison burger? Really? Or elk? She couldn't imagine. Although she might be willing to try the huckleberry pie.

But for now she'd settle for a plain old beef hamburger. Maybe from one of the ranches her Kyle Slater had worked at. Or maybe was working at now.

Telling herself she had to earn her dinner, she turned back to her computer. Grabbed the mouse she used because she hated the inexactness of touchpads and began. Even more determined now—never let it be said she hadn't inherited the Colton stubbornness—she shifted her focus. Widened it beyond location. She set up a new search, this time one that would take some time to run since she had multiple filters applied. She started it, then got up to walk around the room a little while it ran.

If there was a mention of her particular Kyle Slater anywhere online, eventually she'd find it.

Her stomach growled a warning, and she gave in. This search was wide enough she could have a lot of data to wade through, and she didn't want to do that when she was hungry and tired. It might only be 8:00 p.m. here, but her body clock thought it was 10:00 p.m. She made her room service order—definitely the beef hamburger—and was surprised when they told her it would be there within twenty minutes. Yes, this was not a thousand-room hotel, but still…

When the knock on the door came eighteen minutes later, she was impressed. She tipped generously—as a teen she'd spent a summer waiting tables once, and had developed a greater appreciation for service personnel—making the young woman who'd so nicely set her up smile. That encouraged Ashlynn to ask about cab service in the area.

"My brother's a ride-share driver, if you need to get somewhere," the woman—Brianna according to her name tag—said. Then, with a grin, she held out a business card and added, "I can't offer this unless someone asks. But you did, so here's a card with the local number, so you can ask for him."

Ashlynn smiled back at her, relieved. She'd half expected there to be no such thing around here. "Well done," she said.

The grin widened. "Just leave the cart outside when you're done, and we'll pick it up."

The meal was, to her surprise, delicious. A match for anything she'd had in the city and better than many.

Maybe you should stop being surprised. Maybe you should think about why. Prejudiced much?

She set aside the plate with the slice of huckleberry pie she'd decided to try, and wheeled the cart out into the hallway. If it was still there, she'd add the plate later, after she'd eaten the dessert. Or at least tried it.

When she went back to the small desk, she saw her search was still running, but there were already several hits, and a glance told her some would merit further investigation. She knew herself well enough to know she could grab one that looked likely and disappear down another rabbit hole all too easily, so rather than start looking before she had the complete results she decided to check messages. She had, at the insistence of her brothers, temporarily deactivated her personal cell phone. But she could still access any texts via her secure and protected connection on the laptop.

She opened up the messaging app and checked it. The first three messages were from friends she'd let know at the last minute that she'd be out of touch for a while, on business. They all knew she worked for the FBI, but only one knew her true assignment, with the team specializing in serial killers. She'd known Lisa since before her father had been murdered by one, so her friend understood quite well why she did what she did.

She resisted the urge to answer. She'd told her brothers it would be safe, that if anybody tried to track the source it would come back that she was at home in New York, but they were adamant—and Cash had pointed out the less her friends knew, the safer they'd be—so at last she'd given in and promised.

She checked on her search. It was still running. There were apparently a lot more Kyle Slaters then she would have guessed. She glanced at the time. Immediately translated the 9:30 to 11:30. She briefly thought about taking a nap, postponing going through the results until she'd slept a little.

"Yeah, right," she muttered aloud to herself. "Like you could do that."

She moved to close the message app. Stopped in the instant before she clicked when the chime announcing a new message sounded. She reversed course and went back to click on the new message. Her mind registered that it was from an unknown sender, but her finger was already committed. The new arrival popped open.

You can't hide from me. I'll find you.

A chill swept her, but it was followed by a wave of fury. Knowing that here on her well-hidden laptop, unlike on her phone, she was protected from him finding her location, she angrily tapped out an answer.

I'm smarter, and no you won't.

The moment she sent it the anger was overtaken by the caution that should have risen first. She wasn't supposed to engage with this psychopath, under any circumstances, safely hidden or not.

She waited, holding her breath.

Nothing happened.

But he always answered, at least once. Sinead said it was part of his psyche, a need to always have the last word.

The screen remained unchanged.

Her mind began to race. Why didn't he come back

with a retort, as usual? Had she struck a nerve? What would he do? Had she unintentionally escalated things with her angry, instinctive response? Would he move faster now? Maybe he'd kill the next two people, the *O* and the *L* of O'Leary, in one spree?

Her stomach churned.

What had she done?

Chapter 4

"Slater! I need to talk to you!"

The shout came from the other end of the big barn, where the ranch office was. And Kyle knew the voice.

The boss. The big boss, not just Matt. No, that voice belonged to Matt's father, James Wesley, who owned the whole darned place.

Crap. Now what? Had he screwed something up? He knew he hadn't with the horses, he never did. He'd grown up caring for them, and loved them as much as he loved anything. It was the people stuff he usually messed up. His father had seen to that.

He gave Splash—damn, he was going to miss this horse—a final pat and stepped out of his stall. After securing it, he turned and headed down the wide aisle of the barn. Other equine heads popped out as he walked. They watched him, several nickering softly.

Still trying to think of what he might have done

wrong to merit the ranch owner's attention, he came to a halt before the imposing man in the Western suit, black cowboy hat, and boots polished to a high gloss. He doubted his own worn, scuffed boots would look like that if he spent a week and a gallon of shoe polish on them.

"Sir?" he asked, his tone wary as he mentally tightened his grip on his temper, although he had that down to a science now. The only thing that really triggered it anymore was someone hurting an animal, and he doubted he'd ever rein that in.

Mr. Wesley nodded back the way Kyle had come, toward the horses who were still watching. "They like you."

Well that was unexpected. "I like them."

Mr. Wesley nodded. Then he said, "I wanted to talk to you about the Fishers."

Uh-oh.

He'd done his best with the kid yesterday, and had thought he'd gotten him to open up a little as they rode along and he described things as they passed. The boy hadn't cared much about bushes or trees, but had reacted with at least awareness to the animals he pointed out, from rabbits to a pair of coyotes ranging in the distance. But especially to the prairie dog colony he'd purposely guided them past. Judging by that, after their ride he'd taken him in to meet Splash. He'd actually gotten a wide smile out of the boy when the colt had reached down to nudge the little human who was smaller than any he'd met before. The Appy might be wary of adults, and skittish around them, but the little ones he seemed to like. Or at least not see as a threat.

Odd, he thought suddenly. He'd said almost the same thing to the boy as Mr. Wesley had just said. "He likes you." Which had widened the smile even further. He'd actually felt an unusual sense of satisfaction, of accomplishment at having succeeded, for a few minutes at least, at breaking through the grief.

But then, he knew a little about grief, and how all-consuming it was.

He scrambled now to try and remember if the parents had seemed upset over anything, if they'd said anything to him that might explain this. He couldn't think of anything.

"I received a call from Glen Fisher last night."

Damn. He called to complain?

But Mr. Wesley was smiling. Nodding. "He wanted to thank me for a wonderful day, especially for their little boy. Said the child is more himself than he's been since their other boy died."

Kyle could breathe again. "Oh. I'm glad."

"He also said that was mainly because of you. That you handled him perfectly, and that he hasn't stopped talking about you and that colt you introduced him to, and this when he'd barely spoken at all for six weeks."

Kyle felt a tightness in his chest it took him a moment to recognize as pure emotion. The kid had seemed so closed off, so lost…and he'd changed that? He didn't have the words for how that made him feel, wasn't sure there were any. The only thing he was sure of was that he'd never felt it before.

"I…thank you. For telling me." He didn't know what else to say.

"No, thank you. I do business with Glen occasionally, and having him pleased with their time here will pay off for us in the long run." He smiled then. "And for you right now." He reached into his jacket pocket and pulled out an envelope and handed it to Kyle. "They left you a tip. Suggested you deserve a raise, which is probably true. But I'm afraid that isn't in the budget at the moment, so instead...would you be interested in taking over the foreman's cabin?"

Kyle blinked. If there was one thing he liked least about this work, it was living in a communal bunkhouse where the noise stopped late and started early. Sometimes in the summer when it was warm enough at night, he made up a bedroll and slept outside, just to have a night of peace. The others thought him a little strange, or at least different, but...he was.

He knew the cabin, just the other side of the main pasture, and that it had once been the ranch foreman's, before he'd retired and Matt had taken over. Although half the size, it had almost the same feel as Kyle's favorite place, the cabin up in the foothills that rarely got rented to guests because of its remoteness.

The foreman's place was a bit rustic outside, and not far from the bunkhouse but...separate. Inside he knew there was just a living room and one bedroom and bathroom, with a small kitchen alcove, but it was private. It might not have the big-screen TV that was in the living area of the bunkhouse, but he wouldn't miss it that much. As long as he could read, in blissful silence, he'd be happy.

"That would be great, sir."

"It's all yours, then," he said. "Better check it for problems, though. It hasn't been occupied in a while."

"I don't care if it's been occupied by prairie dogs," he answered, rather fervently.

"At least they're quiet at night," Matt said, and a grin flashed across the man's usually serious face. Kyle couldn't help it, a single laugh escaped him, and then a smile.

As his father walked out of the barn and headed back to the main house, Matt studied him for a moment before he said, "Don't think I've ever seen you smile like that." Kyle shrugged, embarrassed. "I know the shared space got to you," Matt added.

A probable realization struck. "Was this your…did you suggest this to your dad?"

Matt shrugged. "I might have mentioned it."

"I…thanks."

"I get a good worker, I like them to stick around."

Stick around.

Normally the thought of staying anywhere made him twitchy. But now, between Splash and this new development…maybe he wouldn't bail when that deadline rolled around.

"Take the afternoon and get your stuff moved."

That'll take me about five minutes. Kyle grimaced inwardly, thinking of his few belongings. It would take him longer to move his borrowed library books than all his possessions.

"Let me know if you need anything for repairs," Matt went on. "Oh, and pay more attention to that phone of yours, since I'm not going over there every day to do a rerun of the bunkhouse spiel on what's on for the day."

"Yes, sir. Absolutely," he promised. *I'd better find that charger…*

He headed for the bunkhouse, only thinking just before he got there to stop and open the envelope Mr. Wesley had left for him. He reached for the flap, thinking maybe ten bucks. That would buy a couple of e-books he'd had his eye on. Twenty, and he'd borrow the ranch truck and head into Bozeman to pick up a couple of things he needed to replace.

Rein that in, Slater. You were only doing your job, after all.

He reached into the envelope, pulled out the contents. And stared at the hundred dollar bill in shock.

He'd known they were well-off, but…wow. His mind wanted to race, thinking of what he could do with this windfall, but he made himself focus on the task at hand. He didn't have all that much to move. A big duffle bag and his backpack held everything he owned. He'd long ago learned to let go of things, because they only slowed you down. Because of that he doubted it would take him even an hour to get himself moved, and so plenty of time to check the building for those prairie dogs.

Better them than black-footed ferrets, who really would be up all night making noise.

And as he gathered his things, he couldn't help smiling at the thought of a peaceful quiet night. Some of it spent deciding where that unexpected but very welcome hundred would go.

And some of it he might really have to spend thinking about delaying his mentally scheduled departure.

Ashlynn had fallen asleep almost unknowingly. She'd simply thought she couldn't keep doing this any longer, pacing the floor of her room because she was too nervous to just sit and watch that messaging screen for a text that never came. She'd sat down on the bed, then swung her feet up and leaned against the headboard. And that was the last she remembered.

The last reality, anyway. Her unplanned sleep had included plenty of images she would just as soon forget.

She couldn't stop herself from checking the messaging app again. Still no response to her impulsive, taunting and most of all foolish answer. This time when she thought if she was in the field she'd be dead by now, it wasn't a joke at all.

With a self-condemning sigh, she closed it and went to look at her search. It had finished an hour ago, and she'd slept right through the notification sound. She supposed that meant she really had been tired.

On that thought she had to stifle a yawn. *Never underestimate the power of suggestion when it comes to yawning.*

She called up the results, set them to sort according to date. Yawned again, glanced at the small coffee maker on the counter, but instead got up to grab another soda. She preferred the carbonation for the kick, when it came to waking herself up. Besides, she was spoiled when it came to coffee, preferring the more elaborate brews she could get at any of the dozen shops within walking distance of the office in the city.

She sat back down, yawned once more, took a large swallow out of the can she held. The kick and the cold did the job, and her eyes were clearer when she looked at the screen.

She eliminated the first three entries right away, since one was an obituary of a seventy-eight-year-old man in Chicago, one was a news story on a teenage football phenom in Kansas and one was a correction to a story that had referred to a man named Lyle as Kyle by mistake.

The fourth she considered, since the age was about right, but the likelihood of the man she was looking for being a real estate salesman in San Diego seemed slight.

The fifth item, from of all things a review site, stopped her dead. Her brain registered the factors in rapid succession. A ranch, albeit a dude ranch. The Double W. She couldn't decide if the name was catchy, or silly. She went back to reading.

Not far outside of Bozeman. Owned by one James Wesley. Managed by his son, Matt. *There's the double W*s.

The review described the place as beautiful, authentic, well-kept and welcoming. Five stars out of five. With a special shout-out to a particular employee there. A man who had gone over and above to help their grieving young son, reaching him in a way no one else had been able to since their other son's death in a tragic accident. A man who had been kind, patient and understanding, and had seemed to know just what to say and do.

A man named Kyle Slater.

Chapter 5

Ashlynn—Zoe, she reminded herself yet again—had always thought horses beautiful. Of course, the closest she'd ever been to one was the occasional encounter with a carriage in Central Park or a mounted police officer in the city. And that had always been at a distance. So somehow she'd never realized how...alive they were.

Big, yes, she'd known that obviously, but now, up close to the one who had curiously come up to the fence as she passed, close enough to feel the heat radiating from it, hear the faint sound as it reached its nose out to sniff at her, to watch the alert ears swivel in a way she'd never noticed before, and most of all to look into the big, gleaming brown eyes...she felt almost silly at how she'd come to think of them as somehow different than other domesticated animals.

Be honest, you were thinking like they were robots

*or something. Because they let us humans use them for
so many things.*

"Ms. Lamont? If you'll come inside we'll get you
checked in."

"Of course," she said, surprised at how much she
wanted to look at the horse some more. But she needed
to be alert, paying attention, now that she was here at
the dude ranch—or guest ranch, they apparently called
it these days—where the hard-to-track Kyle Slater
worked. Unless he'd left since early this morning, when
she'd gotten that hit.

She thought about simply asking for him by name
at the desk, but that seemed a bit blatant. It just didn't
seem wise to give him any warning that she was here to
find him, because of his connection to Xander. And she
was being extra cautious right now, after her impetu-
ous response to the Landmark Killer's text. The text he
still hadn't responded to. Nor had there been any more
killings. Whoever the *O* in O'Leary was going to be, it
hadn't happened yet.

Not Xander. Surely not Xander.

The staff was quite polite, giving her brochures of
available activities when she said she wasn't sure what
she wanted to do yet, and once she'd signed that name
that wasn't hers on the registration form, she and her
bags were in an electric cart—she laughed at the realization she'd almost hoped for a horse-drawn buggy of
some kind—and on her way to the cabin she'd rented.

She felt pleasantly surprised when she stepped inside. The log exterior had been rustic enough that she'd
thought, with some dread, that this might be more camp-
ing than anything, but the fixtures inside were modern
and sleek, and all the mod cons were there, from flat-

screen to a high-end—hooray!—coffee machine. Even the desk was more conducive to her work than the hotel had been, it had room to accommodate her pull-out second monitor and more space for her beloved mouse.

Once her bags were inside—she never surrendered her tech bag to anyone, even though it was heavy—and she was alone, she took a moment to study the coffee machine and programmed it to start. She checked the burner phone for any updates—still quiet on the Landmark front—then began to set up. The connection was solid, which had been another worry, and she double-checked all her masking and security protocols before she signed in.

She'd made this move in such a rush, fearing she'd lose the trail, that she hadn't taken the next step and run a wider search on the name in conjunction with this location in case there was more data. She set that going now, adding in the parameters of Kyle Slater's hometown of Elkton, and his and Xander's father, Victor. Normally she would have done all this before ever leaving the city, but things were hardly normal right now.

Face it, normally you wouldn't have left the city at all.

She launched her widened search, then started to unpack. Her wardrobe ran more to things suitable for work and the city, so every more casual thing she owned had come along. Including the designer jeans she'd bought this last summer, a couple of her warmest sweaters and her second-warmest winter coat. She'd spent Christmas in Montreal one year, and it was at about the same latitude, so she was guessing the weather might be at least similar. Meaning cold, in October.

She'd turned to her friend Laura, who'd grown up in

Wyoming, for advice on shoes; it was the Cowboy State, after all. She'd said the jeans would pass—barely—but had laughed out loud at her idea of boots.

"You'd break your ankle just walking through a barn on those heels, honey. Take those sheepskin things of yours instead. What brought this on, anyway?"

She'd silently called herself every synonym for stupid she could think of. She should have known Laura would ask, and should have had a bland, vague answer ready. But instead she'd burbled out something stupid about a trip her brothers had given her. She clearly wasn't cut out for this secretive stuff.

But Laura had, since they wore the same size, loaned her a pair of actual cowboy boots that she found surprisingly comfortable. And while it wasn't her style, she could appreciate the detail work of the carved black leather. She even liked that they obviously weren't brand-new; at least she wouldn't look as if she'd just hit some Western store on her way here.

"Face it, you are the proverbial fish out of water here," she muttered as she pulled on the beloved sheepskin boots she had indeed brought, and felt the familiar soft hug of warmth.

She picked up the brochures they'd given her and scanned them. To her surprise, a couple of things piqued her interest. The riding basics classes, followed by trail rides she'd have expected, and she had to admit that judging by some of the amazing photographs of what they'd see, they were tempting. She appreciated a beautiful natural setting as much as anyone; she'd just never felt the drive to live in one. Her mouth quirked into a wry, one-sided smile. She was too spoiled, having everything at hand, and the idea of having to get in a car

and drive simply to get her favorite latte just didn't reso-
nate. She much preferred riding the elevator down and
walking two doors away.

But the photos of the wildlife made her smile, and she
thought it might be worth it to see a prairie dog village,
or actually see an eagle in flight over its natural habitat. She grimaced. The snakes, however, she could do
without. And a wolf in person would likely terrify her.

Her laptop again sounded the cheerful notification
she'd assigned to the end of a search. She tossed the
brochures down on the bed and walked back over to
the desk. She started her usual routine, looking for
items that were obviously not connected and eliminat-
ing them. Then she'd go back and start from the top,
going through—

The first item that hit all her parameters caught her
attention. Normally she'd continue her process of elimi-
nation, but something in the intro stopped her, and she
clicked on the result. She started to read. A few seconds
later she was staring at the screen in shock. In even her
wildest imaginings, she never would have expected the
thread-thin trail to lead to this. In her efforts to help
track one murderer, she'd apparently stumbled right
into another.

She read the story again, a grim tale about the brutal death of a young woman who had been pushed into
a traffic lane and crushed by a passing semi. The first
suspect had been, as she would have expected, her boyfriend. But his alibi had been rock solid and unbreak-
able; he'd been in Helena, nearly a hundred miles away,
picking up a horse for his then boss. There was security
video of him gassing up the truck at a station just outside of the capital city at the time of the murder.

In the end, it was the father of that boyfriend who had been convicted of the gruesome crime. The testimony of that boyfriend, who spoke of his father's brutal streak, of how many times he himself had been beaten badly enough to end up in the emergency room. And of how that father had hated the victim, and threatened her more than once.

The father was in prison now.

The father named Victor Slater.

And the character witness son had been Kyle Slater.

Xander wasn't even mentioned in the story, he had been years gone from Montana by the time this had happened. And she knew murderers didn't necessarily run in a family, but….the question mark in her mind about the man she'd thought of as a friend grew larger in her mind, and practically started to glow.

Chapter 6

Ashlynn was still wrestling with herself half an hour later, pacing the floor of her cabin. She knew she had to tell the team what she'd learned, but she also knew what would happen when she did. They would demand she return home where they could protect her.

She glanced at the clock on the nightstand. It was just past noon, so just after two back home. She had time to think a little, before she told them. She wanted to see if she could find Kyle Slater first, see if she could get a feel about him. After what had happened to his girlfriend, and at such a young age, not to mention that he'd testified against his own father, she doubted he was involved in any way. But it couldn't hurt to be sure.

At least that's what she told herself as she secured her laptop in the room's safe. She slipped off her soft boots, changed into jeans, and pulled on the borrowed boots. She stepped out onto the small porch. It was chilly, but not truly cold since it happened to be a relatively clear day. Still, she went back and grabbed her favorite pull-over sweater and slipped it on. Deciding it would be enough, she locked and left the cabin, stuffing the key in her jeans pocket.

She stopped a few feet from the cabin and looked around, still amazed by all the open space. The biggest patch of open ground she frequented was Central Park, so this was…unnerving. Even the mountains were huge. She'd been to the Adirondacks, but these seemed almost twice as high and ten times as forbidding.

She saw a large barn off to her right, where there seemed to be a couple of people working. She started that way. The first thing she really noticed was that the boots Laura had lent her really did make it easy to walk on this uneven ground. Well, uneven to her, used to side-walks. The second thing hit her when she took a deep breath. The unusual scent of…nothing familiar. No whiff of pretzels or coated nuts from a street vendor, no smell of hot dogs from a cart, no pleasant wash of clean laun-dry scent. But none of the less pleasant odors, either, no urine, day-old fish or unidentifiable scents coming out of the building vents as you walked past. It took her a few more steps to realize what she was smelling was clean, brisk air, tinged with the fresh touch of evergreens.

And then as she neared the barn, she at last got a fa-miliar scent. All those visits to Central Park had accom-plished this, at least. She recognized the odor of horse manure. It made her smile, and that it did made her smile wider. Who'd have ever thought she'd welcome that particular smell?

She paused beside the older man who was hitching a pair of lovely horses to a wagon just outside the barn, she supposed preparing for one of the hay rides she'd seen in the brochure.

He glanced up when she stopped. He had bright blue eyes that were striking with the silver of his hair. The kind of eyes that looked as if they'd seen more than most.

"Looking for something?" he asked politely, after introducing himself only as Elliott.

"Is it all right to go into the barn?" she asked.

"Of course," he said. "We recommend you don't touch any of the horses until you're properly introduced, though."

She supposed they had to be careful about that, but the way he put it made her smile. "And who's the lucky person who gets that task, introducing newbies?"

He smiled back. "Any of the hands can do it. I think Jolene is around. Or Kyle's in the barn. He's your best bet anyway. He'll be in the last stall on the right, with the colt. I think he's in love with that little guy. And vice versa, since Kyle's the only one he'll behave for."

Kyle.

Well, that was almost too easy.

"Anyway, if you want to know anything about the horses, he's the one to ask. Guy knows more than the rest of us put together."

She thanked him and started toward the barn, what he'd said about the man being in love with a baby horse making the smile spread to the inside. When she reached the partially open large sliding door she was struck by a new, unfamiliar scent. She would have expected something similar to the droppings she'd smelled outside, but this was different; this whole thing was different than she'd expected. The predominant smell was what had to be hay, spiced by a sweet aroma she connected to the large sack of some kind of grain she saw in a wheelbarrow just inside the door, and on the edge of it all a touch of what had to be leather, oiled and cared for, and something else she couldn't name.

But most of all, the place was alive. The rustling of hooves in straw—she saw a couple of bales of the yellow stuff at the far end—the occasional soft nicker or snort…and that was it, that was what she hadn't been able to categorize. It was the scent of the horses themselves, warm, breathing, unique.

She took a step inside and looked around. A very wide aisle ran down the middle between two rows of stalls, at least a dozen each. She was able to classify some of what she saw, like the trunk full of brushes and combs and what she guessed was a scraper to get mud and dirt off the horses, the halters hanging outside each stall and the wheelbarrow with the bag she now saw was labeled Sweet Feed. For some reason that made her smile, too. And she realized she'd smiled more since she'd stepped outside her cabin here than she had in months. The Landmark Killer case had really been wearing on her.

Some of the other things she had no idea about, the various hooks on the walls, the fact that some stalls had tall walls between them and some only short, and why a few of the top doors were closed. She also noticed a clipboard outside almost every stall, with a pencil attached with a string. She supposed it was to track anything about the animal inside, and after a moment's thought she could see why it was necessary; with several different people dealing with the animals, they had to keep records. But pencil and paper? Could it get any-more low-tech than that?

She noticed that the first space on the left was not a stall but an office, with a small desk and chair on the far wall. There, at least, was a computer. That was comforting.

The corresponding space on the right was apparently where they kept saddles and bridles and other such gear, and according to the small sign above the door, was called the tack room. Why, she had no idea. Tack? Were things tacked to the walls? Or maybe it was short for tackle, like people who fished called their gear tackle. She didn't know the source of that, either. Before the Landmark Killer, she would have launched herself into finding out, just because she had an innate curiosity about the origin of such things. But now she couldn't allow herself the time. She was here for a reason, and it wasn't to figure out what tacks had to do with horses.

It was to find Kyle Slater.

She started to walk down that wide space, her intent to search for her quarry. But equine heads kept popping out as she went, and she couldn't seem to resist looking at each one. There was a gray one there, with a mixed gray and black mane, a brown one with a black lock of hair hanging down over its forehead and a reddish one over there with a mane that was a sort of strawberry blonde that made her smile again. She was sure there was a name for each coloration—humans were good at that, naming and classifying everything—but this was so not her bailiwick she had no idea. Once you got past palominos and pintos, which she only knew from watching a parade now and then, she had no idea.

She'd known she'd be a fish out of water here, but she hadn't expected to feel quite so ignorant. And yet at the same time she felt, not comfortable but…welcomed?

As if all the horses whose heads popped out were curious about her. Maybe she should be feeling inspected instead.

It was strange, how she wanted to go to each one, to meet each one....*don't touch any of the horses until you're properly introduced.*

The warning echoed in her head, and she figured it was probably wise. Horses might not have fangs like dogs—or wolves—but she had the feeling they could still administer a healthy bite if provoked. Not to mention probably kick their way out of these stalls if they really wanted to get to you.

Now, you're being silly. A place like this wouldn't risk having a horse like that around, at least not where a greenhorn like you could get to it.

That was the word, wasn't it? Greenhorn?

She took in a deep breath, surprised at how much she liked this rather unique scent. She had a laughable vision of some perfume shop in the city carrying something trying to duplicate this. They'd probably call it Equestrienne or some such, and as crazy as tastes were these days, it'd probably sell like those food cart pretzels.

She started walking again, trying to think like one of her brothers would, about how she could use this, all of this, to find out what she needed to know. After all, she wouldn't be faking her interest in meeting all the horses, she'd actually felt it, for real.

If you can get them to believe you really understand, that's half the battle.

Cash had told her that once, talking about interviewing a distraught witness. So maybe, if she let her true interest show, it would have the same effect? If Kyle

Slater believed she was truly interested in the horses, he would open up about…other things?

She grimaced inwardly. She was no good at this one-on-one, face-to-face stuff. Give her a screen and a chat box any day. But she had to try. It was the whole point of being here, the whole reason she'd taken Xander's one-time mention that he'd grown up in Montana and hated it, and run with it.

She kept walking, looking.

…he'll be in the last stall on the right, with the colt.

She picked up her pace a little, and moved to the right, then changed her mind, veered back and lightened her step; she wanted to get a look, if possible, before he saw her.

When she got opposite the stall, which like most of the others had the top half of the door open, her breath caught. She might not know much about horses, but that was a beautiful animal. She'd never seen coloring like that, the dark in front so glisteningly black, the white so dazzling, and matched by the white of the stripe that ran down his face, from just above his half-closed eyes to down over his nose to his upper lip.

"Hello, pretty boy," she whispered, unable to stop herself.

As if he'd heard her—did they hear as well as dogs did?—the young animal's head came up sharply, bright, intelligent eyes wide open now. In almost the same instant, a man she hadn't seen straightened up from behind the horse, a brush in his hand.

Hello, pretty boy.

She nearly gasped, in fear that she'd repeated the words aloud. But Lord, did they fit. She'd always had a weakness for that rusty-brown shade of red hair, but combined with that strong, masculine jaw, a perfectly shaped nose and a delectable-looking mouth, it was almost too much. Throw in a pair of gorgeous big dark brown eyes with lashes so thick and long she could see them from here, and it was closer to overpowering.

"Hi," he said. "Looking for something?"

No, I found it. Him. You.

And in that stunned moment the only thing she could think was that it was true, what people said. Driver's license photographs were awful. Because the one of him she'd seen had been utterly nondescript.

Kyle Slater in person was anything but ordinary.

What have you gotten yourself into, girl?

Chapter 7

The woman just stared at him, making him nervous.

"Are you all right?" he asked, although he wasn't sure what he'd do if the answer was no. She was obviously physically all right—okay, more than all right, with that long, dark hair, pretty eyes, cute face and the nice curves—which left mentally. Or emotionally. And the last thing he wanted to do, now or ever, was deal with an emotionally upset female. He was just no good at it. Sarah had once told him—

He snapped off that well-worn mental thread before it could spin out too far. But there was something unsettling about the way the woman was just…staring at him. Still.

"I'm sorry," she said in a rush, as if she felt flustered. "I was just…he's beautiful. The horse."

He relaxed a little. That, he could deal with. "Yeah, he is. He's going to be really something, when he's full grown."

She walked over to the stall door. Kyle noticed Splash didn't try to back off, as he usually did when a strange adult approached. Interesting.

"He's not?" she asked.

He laughed. Maybe she thought Splash was a pony or something. "Nope. He's just a yearling, so he's got a ways to go yet. Or more than a little, judging by the length of his legs."

"Is that how you judge?"

"Roughly. Most horses end up twice the length of their legs in height. So he's got another hand, maybe more, to go."

"Hand?"

Okay, she was definitely a neophyte. "A hand is four inches."

Her brow furrowed. He kind of liked the way a loose strand of hair fell over her brow when she did that. "Let me guess…that's the average width of a man's hand?"

But definitely not stupid. And definitely cute. "That's how it started, so they say."

She looked back at Splash. "But he's already taller than that."

He realized she was looking at the colt's head and explained. "Horse height is measured from their withers, not their head." He patted the appropriate spot on the horse to clarify.

"Oh. Okay." She smiled. "Thanks for the explanation."

Damn, that was a killer smile. "You're welcome."

"Could I pat him?"

He eyed her assessingly for a moment. Glanced at Splash for any sign the horse wasn't as calm as he seemed. Found nothing except what seemed to be curiosity in the colt's manner. Unusual, he thought again.

"Just go slow," he cautioned her. "Hold up one hand and let him reach out to you first, then pat his cheek. Then his nose, if he stays calm."

She did exactly as he instructed, and Splash was surprisingly quick to accept her touch. *Or maybe she's just the prettiest human to ever try to touch him.*

He shook off his own silly thoughts and watched carefully. So quickly it surprised him all over again, she was stroking the usually skittish animal's nose, and Splash was not just letting her, he was clearly liking it. Not that he could blame the horse for that.

She looked from the horse to him with a delighted smile. He scrambled for something to say, anything that would slow the sudden increase in his pulse rate.

"You just get here?" he finally got out. "To the ranch, I mean?"

"Yes, this morning."

"Welcome to the Double W, then."

"Thank you," she said, and the smile was even wider, sweeter. "I'm... Zoe Lamont."

"Kyle Slater," he answered automatically, thinking more about that slight hesitation before she said her name. And then about the way she drew in a deep breath when he answered her. What was going on with her?

Maybe the hesitation on the name was because it had changed? Maybe she was recently divorced or something, and going back to her maiden name. He doubted it was because she'd just gotten married, because what new husband would be crazy enough to leave this woman on her own?

"And this," he added because the silence was making him feel even more awkward, "is Splash." He gestured at the colt, and smiled when she laughed. "And be flattered—he doesn't take to everyone like that."

"He looks like he's been splashed, with ink," she said. "Who named him?"

"Well, I sorta gave him that one. He's got an official, registered name that's about five times as long. Too much of a mouthful to say every day."

"So, is that your job, to take care of him?"

"My job's whatever they tell me it is," he said with a shrug. "But we get along, Splash and I, so they let me see to him. It's important that he get handled a lot now, so he's used to it when he's full grown."

"I always wondered why they let us do so much, when in truth they could take us out so easily."

"I think it's called domestication. Or as some say, easy food equals cooperation."

Splash chose that moment to nudge him, poking his nose under Kyle's elbow, on the arm that held the brush.

"Or else he likes being brushed," she said with a laugh. And a nice laugh it was, high but not shrill, and definitely genuine.

"That, too," he agreed with a grin.

"So, do you ride him?"

"No. He's not old enough yet. Mr. Wesley—he's the owner of this place—prefers to wait until they're fully grown, all their bones and joints solid. Around four. It's healthier for them."

"So then it's what, like some rodeo thing, with bucking and all?"

He was used to that question. "No, not at all. Unless it's what they're trained to do."

"They're trained to buck?"

He nodded. "It's a job for rodeo horses, just like

herding cattle or jumping fences is for other horses. But for just ranch horses, if they're handled right, and slowly, that doesn't happen. Used to be the only way, when horses ran wild until captured and broken to ride, but not so much anymore. And never here at the W."

It was one of the reasons he was liking it here; they might be worlds apart in wealth and station, but he and the Wesleys were in perfect tune about how to treat these animals they both loved.

"I'm glad I chose here, then," she said, looking from him to Splash.

"Why? Why did you, I mean? Or maybe I mean why a ranch at all?" he finished, with a wry grimace at his own conversational ineptitude; he didn't have to worry much about what he said around horses and cattle.

Of course, he wasn't used to conversing one-on-one with beautiful women, either.

"I…" She sounded uneasy, then gave a shrug. "It just sounded like fun. I've never been on a ranch before, and I needed to—" She cut herself off, as if she'd nearly said something she didn't want to. "I needed a break," she finished, rather awkwardly.

He was certain that wasn't what she'd been about to say. But something in those deep brown eyes told him whatever she needed a break from was serious. A breakup, maybe? Then the image of the Fisher boy popped into his head, and he wondered if it was something even worse, a death, maybe.

"You should take a ride," he said impulsively. "There's a spot to the north where you get a great view of the Bridger Mountains, especially Sacagawea Peak. It kind of puts things in perspective for you. Gives you peace."

Her eyes widened and he quickly looked away. What

the hell had he been thinking? He was a ranch hand, not some armchair shrink, assuming she was in need of either of those salves.

"Sorry," he muttered. "None of my business."

"No!" She said it quickly, sharply. "No, it sounds wonderful. And I'd love to. It's just… I've never been on a horse before. I'm just a city girl."

Relieved she hadn't taken offense, he looked back at her. "You came to the right place, then. They have beginner classes here, and—"

"Could you do it? Show me how, I mean?" Her mouth, those lovely lips, curved into a self-deprecating smile. "I don't learn well in groups."

"School must have been a chore, then." Damn, what was with him and his mouth today? Had the thought of giving her one-on-one riding lessons blown up his usual guardrails?

To his relief, she laughed. "It was, a lot of the time. But once I got into computers and tech, and started communicating online, it got easier."

So she's a geek? A nerd? Whatever the term was these days. He didn't know, and didn't much care. He had a phone, knew enough to search for things now and then, and use the maps, beyond that he didn't care. In fact, the opposite. What she clearly loved, he avoided.

Well, that ought to calm you down, Slater. "Puts a wall between you and people, huh?"

"Sort of. For me, more like a step back. Time to take a breath. Think before I say something stupid."

Those last words caught him off guard. He'd never thought of it in quite that way. Hadn't he just been chewing himself out for just that, speaking before he thought, and ending up saying that something stupid?

Slater took a deep breath. Teaching a newb how to stay on a horse wasn't his job. Jolene usually took care of the rookies, and well. But when he'd been hired Matt had made it clear the goal over all was to do whatever it took to keep the guests happy, and if they requested someone help them, that's what they got.

He tossed the brush he'd been using on Splash into the bucket that hung just outside the stall door. He gave the colt a final pat on the neck, then walked over and unlatched the lower half of the stall door and stepped out.

"Come on," he said to her. "I'll introduce you to Daisy. She's the gentlest soul you'll ever meet, perfect for your first ever ride."

The smile that lit up her face made him glad he'd decided to do this.

Made him gladder than he should be.

And he caught himself wanting to whistle as they walked through the barn.

Chapter 8

Daisy turned out to be a pretty little bay—Kyle told her that was what the brown coat/black mane and tail combo was called—who greeted her as if she were an old friend when Kyle haltered her and led her out of her stall. She noticed he bent to check the horse's left front leg just above the hoof, then nodded in apparent satisfaction.

"She's so sweet!" she exclaimed when the horse gently swiped the apple slice Kyle had given her off her palm. She'd almost giggled, because she'd been a little wary, but it had tickled more than anything.

"She is," he agreed. "Ms. Daisy, meet Ms. Lamont," he said rather grandly. Then to her he said, "Now, do a little curtsy."

She blinked, hesitated, thinking he must be making fun of her. But he was just smiling that amazing smile, so she did it, although it was more awkward bow than curtsy. And to her amazement, the horse put one front foot forward and curled the other one up off the ground, lowering her front end in a matching bow.

"Oh!" she exclaimed. "I didn't know horses could even do that. Did you teach her?"

He looked a little embarrassed. "Yeah, sort of. I don't feel like I did because she learned it so quick." His voice shifted to an instructional tone. "Couple of basic things. Don't ever sneak up on a horse—let them know you're there. If you're walking to their back end, trail your hand along their side, letting them know. Especially don't come up from behind and touch. Half the injuries from kicks are because of startle responses."

She barely managed not to audibly gulp. "Okay."

"Daisy is better than most. And mares can be a little…finicky, but she's a smart girl."

"Smart enough to deal with total beginners?"

"That's more the sweet coming out. She's especially good with little kids."

"Well that's good, because that's what I feel like right now," Ashlynn said wryly.

"Don't worry. She just likes humans."

"I thought you said she was smart."

The words were out before she could stop them, and she couldn't miss the momentary sharpening of his gaze. She opened her mouth to explain that she was just in a bad mood from work, but stopped when she realized he had even more reason than she did to not care for certain other humans.

His father murdered his girlfriend. It's amazing he trusts anyone. If he does.

"Sorry," she finally said. "I just left a mess behind at

work. Guess I'm not overly fond of some people at the moment."

"What's your work?" he asked.

Looking at him, into those warm brown eyes, she almost forgot her cover story. *Some spy you'd make.* "I... I'm in tech, for a big organization. Do research, mostly."

"Oh."

Something in his voice prodded at her. "Don't like geeks?"

"Some of them," he said. "I'd rather do without, myself."

"The geeks, or the tech?"

"Both." Then, suddenly, both his expression and his voice softened. "With the exception that proves the rule, of course," he said, holding her gaze, implying she was that exception.

Wow, ego much, girl?

She laughed inwardly, and made herself pay attention as he showed her how to saddle up, as he put it. He ran a brush similar to the one he'd been using on the colorful colt over the horse's back, then he got out what appeared to be a foam pad, rather than the colorful saddle blanket she'd expected from movies and TV. He showed her how to place it, forward and then slide it back.

"Make sure all the hairs on her back are going the right way, not pushed back and irritating her."

"I would not want her irritated," Ashlynn said fervently; now that she was up close to the horse, she seemed even bigger.

"Same thing with the saddle. Better to put it forward and slide it back than the other way around."

He looked her up and down in an assessing way that

might have been insulting in someone else, but she got the feeling he had an impersonal reason. She was proven right when he said, "I think this one—" he nodded toward the saddle that sat on a rack outside the stall door "—is too big for you. Hang on."

He walked over to the tack room she'd noticed before, went in, and came out a moment later with another saddle that, to her eyes, looked just like the one on the rack. She eyed it warily. It looked very big. More importantly, heavy.

"Is that supposed to be smaller?"

He smiled, and for a moment she forgot where she was. Did he have to have such a great smile, on top of everything else?

"It's the seat that's smaller. It'll help you stay in place, and not slide around in a saddle too big for you."

"Oh."

The only saddle she'd ever seen up close had been a racing saddle in an exhibit about the Belmont Stakes, the final leg of the Triple Crown. It had been much smaller and lighter than this cowboy saddle. She thought there was another word for it, but she couldn't think of it at the moment. She was having trouble thinking at all, listening to that honey-smooth deep voice, and occasionally risking a glance at those eyes, that jawline…

"—some just sling it over, but I wouldn't much like getting slammed in the ribs by a stirrup so I hook the far one over the saddle horn before I hoist it."

She tuned back in abruptly. How was she supposed to remain detached when his every instruction was for the comfort and well-being of the horse?

"All right," she said, hating how uncertain she sounded. "I'll try."

She did as he'd suggested with the stirrup, then lifted the saddle—which was not quite as heavy as she'd feared, but close—and turned to the horse. How was she supposed to remain impersonal when he stepped in close to be able to grab the saddle if she started to drop it, as she very likely might. Not, to her surprise, because of the weight, but because he was so close he was making her nervous.

Nerves. Not about him, surely. She just wasn't used to being involved firsthand in an investigation. To being with someone connected to a case in real life. That had to be what it was. She spent her time behind that protective screen, the wall, as he'd called it. Facing them in person in the field was an entirely different thing, and she just wasn't used to it.

No, nothing to do with the good-looking cowboy who was standing so close she caught the scent of fresh hay and open air, as if he'd brought both with him.

She got it done, barely. And the moment the saddle was settled on the cooperative mare's back he stepped away, putting a couple of feet of space between them. She found it easier to breathe normally, but missed his warmth.

It's colder here than at home. That's all.

He made herself pay attention as he showed her how the cinch worked, looping the long leather strap he called a latigo through the cinch ring twice, and then fastening it off into a neat, flat knot.

"She's good about it. Some horses get touchy, they'll tense their abdominal muscles so you think you have it snug, but then when you put weight on the stirrup so all of a sudden it's loose and the saddle slides sideways."

Her eyes widened. "What do you do about that?"

He shrugged one shoulder. "Don't cinch them tight at first. Then do something else, like brush a bit more, or pick out their hooves, until they relax."

"Pick out?"

He nodded. "Any dirt, straw, but especially any stones he—or she—might have picked up. Then you make sure you've got the cinch tight enough, because your weight in the saddle will push it down a bit more, so it'll be looser once you're aboard anyway."

As he spoke he pulled something out of one of the back pockets of his jeans. That, she told herself, was the only reason she was standing there looking at his backside. She wouldn't be, if he hadn't called attention to it by pulling out that…whatever it was, that metal thing with a hook on the end.

"You can try this later, if you want. She's good about the hoof pick, too."

She didn't realize what he meant until he bent down next to the horse's left shoulder and tapped the back of her leg gently. She tore her gaze away from that back pocket and stared in amazement as the animal lifted that leg for him. He caught the front of the hoof and pushed it back slightly, and she saw the bottom of a horse's hoof for the first time. She saw immediately by the shape and contour that it wouldn't be hard for the animal to get a small rock wedged in there. And she quickly realized the tool he'd taken out was for just that, picking out things like that.

She watched, fascinated.

"Lighten up, nag," he said after a moment, but he was grinning when he said it. The horse snorted and shifted, and only then did Ashlynn realize she'd been leaning, forcing Kyle to take a lot of her weight.

She nearly laughed out loud, both at the horse's antics and Kyle's grin; not only was it a killer grin, but it showed how much he cared for the animal. Some men might get irritated and snappish, but he was teasing and light, and the horse reacted in kind.

"She got a little scraped up a couple of weeks ago, so she's been lazing around. Built up a lot of sass, I think. She's a sweetheart, but still a horse. I might have to take the edge off her before you mount up."

"Okay," she said, not exactly sure what he meant but not liking the idea of a sassy horse for her first ever ride. "But she's okay now?"

"Yeah, took the bandage off today, and she's good to go."

She watched him do the hind feet, something she thought looked infinitely more dangerous, with all that hindquarters muscle right there. Then he showed her how to check the cinch again, and gauge that it was tight enough.

When he reached for the bridle—she knew that much, at least—it looked excessively complicated, with all the straps and rings and fastenings. It must have shown in her face, because he quickly explained. "Browband here, noseband here, both just what they sound like. Cheek piece the same, goes down the side of her cheeks. And this is the throatlatch," he finished, indicating the leather strap that went off the main pieces at an angle. "That's what keeps it from sliding off forward."

"Oh."

"She only needs a snaffle bit," he said, indicating the jointed piece of metal she guessed was the part that went in the horse's mouth. "That's the gentlest bit there is.

She'll actually work with just a hackamore, but I figure it's better to have a little more control today."

"And a hackamore is?"

"Like a halter, only with a nose piece that can apply pressure. No bit in her mouth. I'll show you later, if you want."

He patiently showed her how to put on the bridle, and to her surprise the horse didn't seem to mind that bit of steel going into her mouth at all. In fact she seemed almost to bite at it, as if she were in a hurry to get it on so they could get going. And all the while Kyle talked to the horse, teasingly, almost lovingly. And when she nudged his cheek with her nose, Ashlynn couldn't imagine it as anything but a sign of affection.

So you think he's cute too, do you? Or is it just his kindness, his gentleness?

Because he was both of those, it was obvious. She wondered how he managed to be like this, after what he'd been through. Although she supposed it wasn't any worse than what her family had been through, losing their dad so young. But they'd built on that awful experience, channeling their own pain into building the premier serial killer unit in the agency, trying to prevent what had happened to them from happening to anyone else. She and her family were proud of that, and she thought rightfully so.

So perhaps Kyle had channeled his own grief and anger into doing what he loved best. Because it was pretty clear to her that he loved these horses. She could think of a lot worse things he could be doing with his life.

And in the back of her mind was always the thought that he'd had the strength and the character to testify against his own father. Whether it was a measure of his love for his girlfriend or his lack of it for that father, or perhaps a combination of both, she didn't yet know, but no matter which it was it told her a lot about him.

And for the first time she felt a qualm about what she was doing. Until this moment she'd looked upon it as a necessity, just something that had to be done, like following a lead as far as she could go.

But now she realized he was a good man, a kind one, who deserved better out of life.

Who deserved better than to have her lying to him from the moment they met.

Chapter 9

Zoe Lamont clearly hadn't been lying when she'd said she'd never been on a horse before. She exhibited all the traits, the tentativeness, the hesitancy, the barely disguised fear. For a moment Kyle really wished Jolene had been available, she was much better than he with the newbies and kids.

But she wasn't, he was, and it was his job to keep the customer happy. So he tried to focus on the job at hand. And ignore how much he was enjoying just looking at her, at the way she was bold and hesitant at the same time, the way her mouth quirked and her dark brown eyes lit up when she was truly interested.

Kyle was really glad Daisy was ready to go. She was the best for someone like Ms. Lamont. But he hadn't been kidding when he'd said she'd built up some sass while penned up for her leg to heal. The prancing little sidestep she did going through the gate into the big corral showed that. And Ms. Lamont seemed happy to lean on the fence and watch, as if she were grateful for the reprieve. He wondered why she was doing this at all, if she was that fearful. But he supposed he had to admire her for that very reason; not everyone had the nerve to confront their fears head-on.

He thought it might help if she had a distraction. "Watch her left front foot for me, will you?" he asked the woman who was watching intently. "Let me know if it seems like she's favoring it at all."

"Is that the one that was hurt?"

"Yeah, right below the fetlock. The ankle," he clarified at her blank look, and leaned down to touch the joint right above her hoof. "That joint carries everything on a horse, and something like half the injuries in racehorses are fetlock related. So even though this was just a surface scrape on the pastern, I want to keep a close eye on it."

Daisy danced a little when he mounted up, not bad, but enough to maybe freak out a newbie, especially an apprehensive one. He gave the mare a couple of rounds of the big corral before he started anything trickier, then settled into reminding her what it was all about with some sharp turns, reversals of direction, and some long stretches of backing up. He put her through a few big figure eights with a flying lead change in the middle, and by then she had settled into her usual smooth stride. He couldn't sense even a trace of her favoring that front leg, so he was certain now she was fine.

"That was amazing," Zoe said when he road back to the fence where she was waiting.

It had been some pretty basic stuff to him, but he supposed if you really didn't know anything it might be at least interesting. "She's a good horse. A good scrambler out on the trail, and she's got an easy lope that's like sitting in a rocking chair."

A look of apprehension slid over her face then. "That's not what you expect me to do, is it?"

He let out a short laugh. "No. I think we'll stick to walking for a bit, until you get the feel of it."

"Thank goodness," she exclaimed.

She really was cute. He watched as she came through the gate—carefully closing it after her, he noticed—and started toward them. He also noticed her keeping a careful eye on Daisy's hind end.

"She won't kick," he said. "The worst she'd do if you startled her is dance away. But good for you to think about it, it's wise to watch out on any horse you don't know."

She smiled at that. And he grudgingly admitted she was a lot more than just cute. That smile was killer. He had to refocus himself to remember the basics to tell a beginner.

"Always the left side. Some horses are trained to be mounted from either side, but unless you know that, don't try."

"Why that side?"

"Depends who you ask. Most people say it's tradition, from back when knights and other fighters wore their swords on their left side, and it would get in the way if you tried to mount from the far side. Some researchers say the horse likes it better that way. Some just go with it because it's easier, since you saddle up from that side."

She was looking at him as if he were saying the most

fascinating things she'd ever heard. It was unsettling, but pleasantly. "What do you say?" she asked.

He shrugged. "I'm with Xenophon."

She blinked. "Xenophon…the Greek historian?"

"And soldier. He said a rider should always be able to mount from either side."

She looked at Daisy for a moment, then back to him. "So…if they were in a fight they could get away in a hurry?"

He smiled at how quickly she'd gotten there, and nodded. "Or get back into the fray." He shrugged again. "But it applies here, too, if you ask me."

"I did. So why?"

"In part because it helps the horse develop muscle evenly on both sides. Or think about being on a trail ride and ending up with your horse's left side up against a mountain."

He left it at that, not mentioning the time he'd broken his left ankle and putting that foot in the stirrup had been impossible. No point in telling her horror stories before she'd even mounted up for the first time.

"Oh. That makes sense," she said.

"But for now, we'll stick with tradition. Ready?"

"Okay." She sounded uncertain, but stepped forward.

"You can grab the horn and the cantle—the back of the seat there—but try and use your leg as much as you can, rather than pulling yourself up. Doing that digs into the horse even more."

She glanced at him. She was smiling, although he had no idea what he'd said to bring it on. But he'd take it. Crazy how just her smile got to him.

She didn't do badly, for someone who'd never mounted a horse before. "Just remember," he said, reaching up to take the reins and show her how to hold them, "these are attached to the bit, so any yanking is going to hurt her. Gentle pulls is all she needs, and she's trained to neck rein, so you only—"

She held up a hand. "Info overload here. What's neck rein?"

"Sorry." It had been a while since he'd dealt with an absolute beginner. And that fact that she was so pretty wasn't helping. "You keep the reins loose in your left hand and just lay one on her neck on the side opposite of the way you want her to go. At the same time you add a little pressure with the opposite leg."

"That's a couple of opposites," she protested.

"Think of it like nudging her in the direction you want her to go. The feel of the rein on the right side of her neck moves her left. Then you want the back end to continue the turn, so you nudge it around with your leg."

"Okay, I get it now. Nudge I can do," she said.

He smiled. "Good. So, get the reins about here—" he adjusted them in her left hand, bottom to top, and to about the right spot "—and keep them there. The movement should be all to the sides or gently back, unless you want to yank her to a stop and maybe go flying over her head."

"Ouch!" She grimaced, but laughingly, which made him smile wider. "Why just one hand?"

"You're riding Western, honey, and we're good enough to only need one hand."

The old joke in the Western versus English riding styles battle slipped out before he thought about it. Including the "honey," which somewomen found insulting. And for a moment she just stared at him, and he thought he'd really stepped in it. But then she smiled again, widely.

"And here I thought it was so you could hold a lasso or something."

Relieved, he chuckled. "Yeah, that's the real reason. And opening gates, or reaching for a weapon if you happen upon a rattlesnake or some other nasty varmint."

Her eyes widened. "Rattlesnake?"

"Only venomous snake we've got here in Montana. Mostly it's garters and boas, harmless to people. Just listen for the rattle or watch for that triangle head. They only strike if they feel threatened." He nodded at Daisy. "And she'll warn you, if you're out on a trail. That's where you need to be alert, because she's liable to do a moonwalk worthy of Michael Jackson."

She grimaced. "I'd like to stick to this corral for now, thanks."

"Sure. We'll start out with me leading her around the corral, until you get a feel for things."

He hoped he hadn't scared her off riding free completely. He kind of liked the idea of taking her out on a trail ride one day, showing her some of the places he loved. Which was crazy, given he'd only met her a couple of hours ago. And that he never let himself get too close to anyone, because people never seemed to be who you thought they were. And no one knew that better than he did.

Chapter 10

Daisy was as docile as could be as they circled the big corral, but Ashlynn couldn't help wondering how much of that was Kyle holding her lead. A lot, if she had to guess. He'd calmed her down, hadn't he? And she was a lot more nervous than the horse seemed to be. Although hardly for the same reasons. It seemed contradictory that he could relax her at the same time he was revving up her pulse because she liked the way he moved, the way his hair fell, and most of all the twinkle in those warm brown eyes.

She looked away from him before she did or said something stupid. She focused on the horse's head, which bobbed very slightly as they walked. There was a relaxing sort of rhythm to the movement as they circled the enclosure. She could be quite happy staying at this pace. She certainly had no desire to take off at a wild gallop—this was just fine. Slow, but fine. Fine because it was slow, maybe. Not for the first time she admitted that at heart she was a chicken about anything that didn't involve a keyboard or a mouse.

He led them around the corral along the fence a couple of times, showing her how to sit right, and frequently reminding her "heels down" until it became more normal to her. They made it a couple of rounds without him having to correct her on anything. And then he unfastened the lead line.

"You're fine," he assured her.

"But you'll stay with us?" she asked, not even embarrassed at the edge of panic that crept back into her voice.

"Right here," he promised, and he continued walking alongside the horse's head.

After another circuit, he said, "Try turning to the right."

The alarm flooded back. "What?"

"Start with a gentle signal, and only up it if she doesn't do what she should," he said.

"I don't want to argue with her," she said.

Kyle laughed, and the sound of it eased her fear yet again. "She won't argue—with Daisy it'll just be she's not sure of the command. If you're too gentle, she'll think it's just a casual movement. So it needs to be definite, but not harsh."

"How do I know what's harsh with a horse?"

He thought about that for a moment, then said, "Think of it like being in a crowd, with people brushing against you, versus someone tapping you on the shoulder."

"Oh." That made sense. "Okay."

"Left rein, right leg."

She nodded, sucked in a deep breath and held it while she laid the left rein against the horse's neck and pressed gently but definitely with her right heel and calf.

Daisy immediately turned to the right, not quite ninety degrees but close. Ashlynn's breath came out tangled with a pleased, quiet laugh.

"That was easy!"

"Told ya'," Kyle drawled exaggeratedly. When she looked she saw that grin again, and ended up grinning back at him.

Over the next hour, as she learned how to turn Daisy in all directions and even succeeded in making her back up, the whole process began to make sense to her. She could see how the commands worked, from the horse's point of view. She went from terrified to more relaxed to actually enjoying the ride, even though they never got above a fast walk. Just as she thought it, he asked, "Do you want to try picking up the pace?"

"Now?" Her voice didn't quite squeak, but it was a close thing.

"Only if you want to. A trot's the hardest gait to ride, so if you want to wait and start fresh—"

"Yes," she said quickly. "Please. Tomorrow?"

"Jolene should be free, and—"

"No!"

She told herself the snap in her voice was because he was her job here, he was the whole reason she was here at all. She almost convinced herself, and went on more calmly.

"I mean, I'd much rather you did it. If you can, I mean," she added, suddenly realizing the man had a job here, and probably had other things to do.

"I'll see if I can clear it with the boss," he said.

"I don't want to get you in trouble," she said, feeling a bit anxious now.

"It'll be okay. I think he's kind of happy with me at the moment."

I'd be happy with you all the time.

Ashlynn tried to quash the thought that, unbidden, trampled through her mind. What was wrong with her? Sure, he was gorgeous, but she worked around a ton of good-looking guys and she'd never reacted to any of them like this. Was she really such a sucker for the cowboy vibe?

A cowboy who quotes ancient Greek historians, maybe?

But then he reached out and patted Daisy's neck, and the horse nudged him with her nose. And she realized it was his gentleness and kindness with the animals as much as his looks that appealed to her.

And belatedly it occurred to her that he'd had an out, he could have just said the boss wouldn't let him, but instead he'd agreed to go out of his way to make it happen.

He probably just feels sorry for the city girl, the fish out of water.

· That allowed her to rein in—gads, she was thinking in horse metaphors now?—her unexpected response. Her unwelcome response. For surely it was unwelcome, right? She was here on a case, and he was the reason. It was work. Very important work. That had to be why she was so on edge. She just needed to remember this was a case, and just because she didn't normally do this, the in person contact with a person of interest, didn't mean she couldn't. She was smart, savvy, and had a personal stake in this case, as they all did, if it truly was one of their own.

Reminding herself of that hideous possibility seemed to recenter her, and her determination to find out what she'd come here for returned full force. Feeling a bit easier about it now, she found herself studying him in a different way as they headed back to the barn. She hadn't noticed any great similarity in looks between him and his half brother, but she'd been…distracted. So now she looked, but still didn't find much. The nose, maybe, straight and perfectly sized. His eyes were the same color, but somehow his seemed…warmer? More open? She wasn't sure how to describe the difference. Or maybe she was just giving Xander traits that weren't really there, because now he was under suspicion.

When they were back outside Daisy's stall, the horse stopped before she even had to do anything, clearly aware she was home.

"Such a clever girl," she crooned, patting the bay's neck.

Then she was faced with dismounting. Again as if he'd read her mind, Kyle said, "It's just mounting in reverse. Unless you want to get fancy or showy."

"I just want to get down," she said frankly. "It seems farther from up here."

He smiled. "Just free your right foot, stand in the left stirrup, and lower yourself down."

He made it sound so easy. She did as he'd instructed, but her left leg did feel a bit unsteady as she tried to lower herself, and she quickly straightened it again. She stood there with one foot in one stirrup, feeling stupid. Daisy turned her head to look at her as if she were thinking the same thing.

"My legs feel…wobbly," she said, feeling her cheeks heat.

"Normal after your first ride lasting so long. Here, I'll give you a hand."

He in fact gave her two hands, on either side of her

waist, and he lifted her down from her unintended perch as easily as if she were a child. When her feet hit the ground she tried to turn, but he was still too close. They collided, and she found herself almost pressed against him, looking up into those lovely eyes.

"Sorry," he muttered, and stepped back.

"Don't be," she said, meaning it in more ways than one. "I would have been on my butt if you hadn't helped."

Something different flashed in those eyes then, and she told herself firmly not to think it had been when she'd mentioned her butt. Then he looked away, almost hastily.

"You want to finish this?" he asked, still not looking at her, his voice the tiniest bit gruff.

"Finish?"

"Untack her, brush her before she goes back in her stall."

"Oh. Well, I should, shouldn't I? She did let me ride her, with all my clumsiness."

His gaze flicked to her. "You didn't do badly at all." One corner of his mouth twitched. "Landing was a little rough, maybe."

No, keeping my cool with you practically hugging me was rough.

She managed to laugh despite being unsettled in this new and strange way. And she paid close attention on how to unsaddle Daisy, how to carefully unbridle her so the metal bit didn't bounce on her teeth, and then slip the halter on.

She took the brush he handed her, saying "She won't need much, she didn't work up a sweat out there."

"No, I was the one in the nervous sweat," she said wryly, and was delighted when he laughed.

Far too delighted.

In yet another surprise she found she quite enjoyed the task of grooming the gentle animal, even to the point of repeating the hoof cleaning process, although it clearly wasn't really necessary after merely riding around in the enclosure.

"I always thought horse's hooves were hard all the way through," she said. "And solid."

"Nope. That's why you have to check them regularly. All kinds of things can go wrong, from picking up a stone and developing a bruise, to quarter cracks, to laminitis and a whole list of other things."

He let her lead Daisy back into her stall and unsnap the lead rope. She gave the horse a final pat, finding herself talking to her, telling her she'd see her again tomorrow. And it didn't seem the least bit odd to her.

She stepped out of the stall and carefully closed the door behind her. She turned around to see Kyle standing frozen, staring down toward the far end of the barn, opposite where they'd come in. Automatically she looked that way herself, but saw nothing. She looked back at Kyle.

He was still staring. Disbelieving, almost stunned. With a touch of...fear? His expression reminded her of her own reflection in the mirror the morning after she'd found out her father had been killed in the line of duty, murdered by a serial killer.

Her mind veered sharply off that painful memory, and she spoke quietly.

"Kyle?"

For a moment he still didn't move. She was on the verge of repeating herself, and almost started to reach out to touch his arm, when he seemed to snap out of it a little. He glanced at her.

"I thought I saw...someone I knew." He gave a sharp shake of his head. "Sorry," he went on, still sounding more than a little unsettled, "I have to go."

And that he was gone, striding quickly—almost running—toward the far end of the barn where he'd seen whatever he'd seen. Ashlynn watched him go, her brow furrowed in puzzlement. She was concerned enough about whatever it was that had just happened to barely notice that he looked just as sexy from the back. Maybe more so, given the way those jeans hugged his backside.

But what on earth—or who on earth—had he seen that had so rattled him?

Chapter 11

At this moment Kyle was truly grateful that he'd moved into the separate cabin, where he was now pacing the worn wooden floor. He needed to think, and doing that with the usual noise and chatter that went on in the bunkhouse most of the day as the other hands came and went would be nearly impossible. The loud ones were bad enough, although sometimes the good-natured joking and rowdiness was funny, but it was the nice guys, who'd pick up on his mood and be asking him if he was all right, he wanted to avoid.

Because he wasn't all right. He didn't think he ever had been, not in the way of most people.

Before, to get any peace, he would have had to saddle up and ride out to some distant corner of the ranch, which was always a risk because there was no phone signal. Which he much preferred. But then, if he was needed by the boss, he couldn't reach him, and that put his job at risk. And while the plan was still to move on soon, he wasn't quite ready yet.

He stopped his pacing in front of the small window near the door, which looked back toward the bunkhouse and the barn. He stared at the spot where he'd seen that figure darting out of sight. As if seeking diversion, his mind wandered from the matter at hand to wondering how long Zoe would be staying. He quashed that errant thought quickly. It was none of his business, and he shouldn't be thinking about her when he had other, much more crucial things to think about. Such as the fact that this was the third time he'd caught a glimpse a man who looked shockingly like his father.

It was impossible, of course. But on that ride out to the far pasture yesterday morning, he'd seen someone standing on the far side of one of the ranch trucks. The man had dodged away quickly, vanishing into the grain storage shed, and Kyle had decided it must have been a deliveryman who just happened to bear a resemblance. Then later that afternoon, he'd seen the man again, this time near the bunkhouse. Again he'd quickly darted back under cover of the building, and by the time Kyle got there he was nowhere in sight.

All three times he'd gotten barely a glimpse. But all three times he'd had the same reaction; a fierce knotting of his gut, a kick up in his pulse and a chill running down his spine. Because he knew there was nothing his father would like better than to get back at him for testifying against him in court. And Kyle knew exactly what his idea of payback would be, and it would likely be a lot slower death than being hit by a truck.

But it was impossible. Victor Slater was in prison, where he deserved to rot away the rest of his life. That he wouldn't be there that long was already one of the most painful spots in Kyle's painful life. There was no way his father should have gotten away with being convicted only of a lesser charge instead of the cold-blooded murder it had been. No matter how vehemently his defense attorney had stated it had been a crime of passion, Kyle knew better. And he'd testified to that, in open court. Too bad it hadn't been enough to tip the scales, when all the witnesses knew nothing of the enmity between them.

It was true that it had happened when his father had been angry, but his father was always angry. Especially at the woman who dared make his son happy. And Kyle had heard him threaten Sarah often, and loudly, before he'd actually followed through on the threat and killed her.

But ol' Victor had staged it perfectly. In public, in town, with witnesses around, prodding Sarah into shouting at him—she had always ignored Victor's attacks on her, but his attacks on Kyle with one of his diatribes inevitably set her off. And he'd made sure she was heard by passersby before he turned as if to walk away…in the process shouldering her "accidentally" into the direct path of an oncoming vehicle.

Be a shame if that little tramp of yours got hit by a truck.

The memory of Victor Slater's manic laughter as he'd said those words just the day before it had happened still made Kyle feel sick to his stomach. He should have taken it, and him, more seriously. But Victor had done it so many times, threatened so many things, that Kyle had just written it off as another crazy rant by the man he hated to admit was his father.

The next day Sarah was dead. Exactly as his father had planned.

And he's in prison. So he can't be here.

Maybe he'd been working too hard. He liked it here, so he'd given it his all. And that meant some long, hard days. But that was his idea of a good job, one that ate up his time and concentration so that when night came he fell into bed and slept like the proverbial log. That the people here were mostly nice and friendly was a bonus. Only the occasional recalcitrant or arrogant guest that came through was a problem, easily handled because they were only temporary.

He liked it here maybe a little too much. It was almost time to move on, and he hadn't even begun to look for the next place. Just the thought of packing up and moving on to a new ranch felt exhausting. Half the time he didn't even think about why anymore. It used to be his father and the past, what he'd done and the infamy of it in a sometimes starved for news small town. But now it just felt like something he did. A day popped up on the calendar and he snapped to it like a good little robot, following the plan he'd decided on for no other reason than it was the plan he'd decided on.

Maybe he should restart the clock, now that he had the little cabin to himself. Start his year in place from now. Maybe he could cheat a little and count moving here as moving on, at least in a tiny way.

Like moving fifty yards is moving on, Slater?

Or maybe it was time to get off this merry-go-round, if he was so resistant to the idea all of a sudden. Maybe it was time to settle in somewhere and stay, especially now that he had a boss who was great to work for, and a bigger boss who actually appreciated him—

He broke off his own train of thought abruptly. While he was looking for excuses to stay, his subconscious was sending out imaginary sightings of a man locked up over a hundred miles away. That was sign enough it was time to pack it in here, wasn't it? Some part of his brain knew it was time, even if he was trying to ignore it.

He felt the pressure of the conflicting urges, and for a moment he just stood there in the middle of the small cabin, unable to move. He felt trapped, as he had always felt most of his life. And he didn't know what to do except run. As he always did.

But this time the thought of doing it yet again made his gut churn.

Ashlynn sat at the small table that was serving her as a desk, having to remind herself to blink as she stared at her screen. She'd called up everything she'd found on Kyle Slater before she'd given in to the mad urge to come here to the middle of somewhere to try and find him. That was back when all she'd had to go on was Xander's one-time mention of growing up in what he called this Montana backwater he couldn't get shed of fast enough, with pure loathing in his voice and his expression.

She remembered thinking he'd done a very thorough job of that, since there wasn't the slightest trace of cowboy or even country boy in the urbane, polished assistant to the director of the FBI. Not that she was an expert about such things, city girl that she was. But still, the idea of someone as polished and smart and no-nonsense as Xander coming from these roots was a bit boggling.

But the thought of Xander being their killer seemed even more ridiculous. She reminded herself of what her

brother Cash had once told her about their quarries, serial killers, that they were among the best of the best at
hiding the truth of themselves—and often from themselves—otherwise they didn't survive long enough to
become serials.

She played the moment back in her head, of that look
on Kyle's face when he'd seen...whatever or whoever
he'd seen. There had been no mistaking the sequence
of reactions that had played across his face. He'd gone
from startled to disbelieving to stunned all in the space
of a moment. So stunned he could barely speak; he had
taken off a split second later.

But he hadn't run from whatever he'd sighted, he'd
run toward it. She wasn't sure what that meant, but it
felt significant.

She eliminated her first suspicion, Xander, right off
because she'd gotten the text from the team indicating
he was still in New York. So what could have gotten
such a reaction out of him? Maybe it was an ex he'd
seen? A man like Kyle, that quietly sexy, surely wouldn't
have remained alone this long after his girlfriend's admittedly shocking death. Even given the horror of his
own father being the killer—although according to the
reports it had been more accident than murder—there
must have been someone since then.

That would at least explain the heading toward it,
rather than away. Although Ashlynn didn't like the way
the thought of an ex-girlfriend set off a protest in her
mind.

So maybe it's the current girlfriend.

She let out a disgusted breath, because she liked that
idea even less. What was wrong with her? She'd been

on this ranch less than a day, and she was already tangled up over some random ranch hand?

He's not random. He's why you're here. Try to be a professional about it.

Self-lecture concluded—she didn't know how effectively—she turned back to her screen. Maybe he'd just seen someone unexpected. But would that explain the level of shock she'd seen in his face?

Not to mention that touch of fear she'd seen.

Who on earth would Kyle be afraid of?

Only one possibility came to mind, and it was as improbable as everything else. But she hadn't made it to where she was, a trusted member of the team, by accepting things at first glance. And so Ashlynn did what she always did.

She started to dig.

Chapter 12

Kyle stared down at the rarely used cell phone in his hand.

Make the call, idiot.

He wasn't even sure why he was hesitating. Was it because he wanted to convince himself it didn't matter? That he no longer cared? That he didn't want them to think he was crazy? Or for it to somehow leak to his father that he was worried? Scared?

He was just exhausted, that was all. He hadn't slept well at all last night. He still wasn't used to the new place, he told himself, and almost believed it. But it was hard to think clearly, at least about this. It made him once more wish the cabin was more remote, like the mountain one, that it was far enough out that there would be no cell signal, so no question about whether to make that damned call.

He shook his head sharply, trying to clear out some

of the dull hum that had built. In a couple of hours he was due to ride out and help move the last of the small herd of cattle down from the high meadow, now that they'd seen the last of the mild—by Montana standards, anyway—night temperatures for the year. And he had to be alert and aware, since some of the ranch guests would be with him, and had little to no experience in either riding or the task at hand.

The guests expected the ranch to be a working ranch, but it was no longer theprimary source of income so the herd was a fraction of what it had once been, thankfully for the dudes' sake. But still, the Wesleys took as much care with the animals as they ever had, and Kyle appreciated that.

He put the phone down on the counter, rather more energetically than he should have. They had his number. He'd made sure of that, when he'd had to get a new phone last year. They'd call if anything had happened. Wouldn't they? And something unlikely, like a prison break, would surely have made the news. So if he called, how was he going to feel when he found out he'd been hallucinating, imagining, when he had to admit he'd somehow managed to manifest his fears into an image he would swear was real?

He put his hands down on the counter and let his head sag downward, so weary of this haunting his life. He let his eyes close for a moment, but the nightmare scenes started rolling through his mind instantly, as if they'd been lined up just waiting for this moment of weakness in the walls he'd mentally built to contain them. He didn't know how much longer he could go on this way. But what else was he supposed to do?

He straightened up, and turned so he could lean back

against the counter. He studied the door of his new home, wondering if he should walk right back out through it and do now what he'd been wanting to put off. If he should repack his few belongings and move on right now, even before the year was up.

He supposed his gut reaction of "No!" should be a warning, that he was getting soft, complacent. Still, the thought of going to either of the Wesleys and telling them he was leaving, after they'd been so fair and good to him, seemed even more wrong. It wasn't always that way. His father's case had been headline news in Gallatin County, and a lot of people weren't anxious to hire a killer's son.

He closed his eyes again, clenching his jaw. It had been a long time since it had engulfed him like this, and he hated the helpless feeling it gave him. It reminded him too strongly of when he'd been a little kid, longing to spend time with his father, yet always regretting it— and usually carrying a bruise or two—when he did. It had taken him a while to realize that his father wasn't like other fathers. Most, anyway.

When he realized the pain in his fingers was because he'd wrapped them around the edge of the counter as if he was trying to break off a piece, he sucked in a deep breath. Then he slowly released it, at the same time consciously relaxing both his jaw and his fingers.

You're not that helpless kid anymore.

A sudden sound made him jump.

He'd had himself almost steady again, but the knock on the door he'd been staring at brought it all back in a rush. He glanced at the rifle he carried when riding out in the wilder spots, a classic Winchester 94 Trails End lever-action. It wasn't new, but he'd kept it in good condition, and it was unfailingly accurate. The fact that it easily broke down to fit in a smaller case for his frequent moves was why he'd chosen it, and the rest had been a bonus.

Too many moves.

The words echoed in his mind but he pushed them aside. Looked back at the door.

It's not him. He's still in a cell in Deer Lodge, four counties away.

Still, it took him a moment to brace himself and cross the cabin to the door.

He pulled it open. And stared in surprise at the woman on his tiny porch.

"Ms. Lamont?" he said, beyond puzzled. Not that he minded a pretty woman, even if she was a city slicker, showing up unannounced, but his new digs were far enough from the guest cabins that it had taken some effort to end up on his doorstep. He asked the first thing that popped into his head, given that it was a bit of a hike if she'd come on foot. "How'd you get here?"

"They loaned me one of the little…things," she answered with a vague wave behind her where he now saw one of the ranch ATVs parked. He also now realized, when he saw the movement of her hand, that she was, if not actually shaking, at the least trembling. And now that he got a better look at her, he could see that she looked as exhausted as he felt, her eyes a little bloodshot.

Maybe she's a drinker and she's hungover.

Even as the thought formed he dismissed it. She just didn't have the vibe. And he would know, given his mother's usual escape from the brute she'd made the mistake of getting pregnant by had been alcohol.

"Are you all right?" he asked, fearing she was going to pass out on him or something. What the heck was going on?

"I…yes. No." She let out a compressed breath, then, steadier, went on. "May I come in?"

Wariness spiked through him. Maybe the unsteadiness was just nerves, because she was about to…something. One of the standard topics in the bunkhouse was the occasional female visitor who wanted a little more than help with a horse from one of the hands. And being guys, they had some tales to tell. Some took advantage, some didn't, and each group tended to snipe at the other.

He'd never partaken himself, but only because his last foray into any kind of personal relationship had ended so horribly. Even though his father was in prison, he couldn't quite rid himself of the idea that it would somehow happen again. The man was certainly evil enough to arrange it, if he thought Kyle hadn't learned his lesson.

You're good for nothing, kid, anyone can see it. And that's all you'll ever be.

Not the sort of man who'd bring a woman like this one to his door in search of some kind of fling.

"Ms. Lamont," he began.

"Zoe, please. And it's important. I have something to tell you."

She sounded steadier now, but he had no idea what she could need to tell him that required a trip out here to his cabin first thing in the morning. If it was anything work related—Daisy came to mind, maybe her injury had been worse than he'd thought—they would have called him, surely? But keeping her standing outside in the October chill didn't seem right, so he backed up and gestured her in.

"It's not much," he said by way of warning, "and I just moved in. I'd keep your jacket on," he added, "I have to head out to work in a bit so I didn't build a fire or turn on the heat this morning."

She gave him a smile that looked a bit wobbly, but she left her puffy jacket on as she stepped inside.

He was sure she was used to much more luxurious surroundings than the little cabin with the wood paneled walls and worn wood floor, the tiny kitchen and even tinier bathroom. Not to mention that the minimal furniture, a small sofa, one end table with a lamp, a faded rug between them and the small, old wood stove, and the table that had just enough room for the two chairs, were all timeworn and a bit shabby.

At least he'd closed the bedroom door, so she couldn't see into the equally tiny space, with barely enough room for him to walk between the bed and the single chest of drawers on one wall.

Like you want her peering into your bedroom anyway, making you think about things you shouldn't be thinking about. A shaft of heat shot through him as he looked at her, at that long, silky dark hair, and those eyes that were nearly as dark and with even more shine. And suddenly he was thinking about the size of that bed, and how they'd have to be very, very friendly to sleep in it.

Or do anything else in it, like all the wild thoughts that were streaming through his mind like an X-rated movie.

He knew what had brought this on. It was remembering all that ranch equivalent of locker room talk that had his brain skittering down paths he had no business following. That was all it was. She was a ranch guest, and he a mere ranch hand, and he'd better rein it in.

Even if she had shown up here on his doorstep.

And now she was looking around, but kind of vaguely, as if she weren't really seeing what was there, but something in her mind's eye. He knew that feeling.

"Do you need…something?" He barely managed not to stumble on the words as his imagination tried to take off again. He cleared his throat. Remembering what she'd said, he tried again. "You said you wanted to tell me something?"

And finally she turned to face him. "Yes. It's just… difficult. Can we sit? I've been up most of the night."

He blinked. She hadn't slept either? What on earth was going on here?

"I…sure." He gestured toward the small couch, realized how close they'd be sitting, and wished he'd gone for the table instead. Small as it was it was solid and would be between them.

She sat down, staring at her hands clasped and resting atop knees held primly together, her legs clad in jeans that looked about a century newer than anything he owned. He'd thought she looked tired, although even he knew enough not to say that to a woman. He wanted to ask why she'd been up most of the night, figured he'd manage to bungle the asking and stayed quiet.

But so did she, so he finally had to ask, "What is it, Zoe?"

She looked up then. Met his gaze. Took a deep breath. "Your father was released from prison three days ago."

Chapter 13

Ashlynn had known he would be shocked, and when his first words were "What the hell?" she wasn't surprised.

"It was some kind of deal—I don't have the details yet."

He was staring at her, brow furrowed, clearly astonished. "How the hell do you know about my father? Who are you?"

She'd convinced herself, almost, that the fact that she'd lied to him about herself didn't matter. She had her own reasons that had nothing to do with him—unless Xander turned out to be their serial—and why would he care much anyway? Sure, anyone would likely be irked that someone had lied about their name and why they were here, but there was no reason that should bother her this much. And telling herself it was part of this job—not her specific job, usually, but this one—didn't seem to be helping much.

She should have thought about this more, prepared what she would say when he inevitably asked, but no, she'd plunged right in. Why, when she was usually so cautious in her dealings with other people, especially strangers? The only answer she could come up with was unacceptable. She was careful, not reckless. Cool, not...passionate.

And why was that the word that came to mind?

"Is that even your name?" he snapped when she didn't answer.

"No," she admitted, finally remembering how to speak. "I am here under an alias, but... I can't tell you why."

"Right," he said, his tone sour now.

She could read in his face, in those dark brown eyes that right now seemed deep enough to drown in, that at this moment he didn't trust her as far as young Splash could throw her.

"I can't," she repeated. "It's nothing to do with you—" Well, directly anyway. "It's for my own safety. My family insisted."

"Safety? You're in trouble?"

She wondered why that was what had registered for him. "Not here. I'm safe enough here." *I think.* She took in a breath and tried again. "Look, I know it sounds crazy but you have to trust me. Or if not me, trust that I know what I'm talking about." She nodded toward the phone she could see on the counter. "Call. They'll tell you."

"They're supposed to call me," he said.

"Yes, they should have. I don't know why they didn't."

Even as she said it the phone she'd glanced at rang. Kyle started. The fact that this man who dealt with animals more than five times his weight, and cattle that might weigh even more, both with dangerously hard hooves, would jump at the simple sound of his phone told her something. The only problem was she didn't know if it was because he wasn't used to getting calls, or that he was that much on edge.

Both.

That was her best guess, and she was pretty sure she was right. She might not be able to read people as well as she could interpret data, but he wasn't that hard to interpret, even for her.

"You going to answer that?" she asked when he didn't move.

"Only if I have to."

Distaste was clear in his voice, and she got the impression she hadn't given the first part of her theory, about him not getting a lot of calls, enough weight. Because it looked to her as if he went out of his way to avoid them. To a woman who lived by her phone when she wasn't at a computer, this was…strange. True, she preferred texting to voice calls, but to ignore it altogether did not fit into her mindset at all.

"It could be the prison," she pointed out.

He gave her a sideways glance, and she couldn't miss the unhappiness in that look. Finally he let out a compressed breath and walked over to pick up the phone just as she guessed it was about to go over to voice mail.

He didn't say much at first, after confirming who he was. Certainly not enough for her to be sure it was the prison. But after two very stiff responses of "I understand" and "I see," she was fairly sure.

And finally he confirmed it when he said, a touch of Montana ice in his tone, "Actually I already knew, because he's here, hanging around where I live and work. It would have been very nice not to have had three days of thinking I was losing my mind."

When he hung up he stood there staring at the phone in his hand for a long, still moment. She got up but didn't speak, instead braced herself for what she guessed was coming. And it did.

He turned around to stare at her. "How did you know?"

She diverted, or tried to. "Did they apologize for the screw-up?"

"All over the place. How did you know? Why does my father's name mean anything to you at all?"

"Kyle, I can't tell you."

He gave a derisive snort. "I'll bet. Did you know all along? Is that why you're here?"

"No, I only just found out, I swear." He shook his head in disbelief. She pushed on. "They didn't know where he was? That he was…here?"

"They told me he missed the first check-in with his parole officer, so he's already in violation. That's the sum total of what they knew."

"Kyle, I'm sorry—"

"Are you—" he looked her up and down, the disbelief clear in his voice as well "—what the Department of Corrections sends out looking for escapees these days?"

She would have taken offense, if she'd had any ground to stand on. But she knew quite well she was hardly the type to be sent out hunting down a killer. No, that was left to her field agent twin brothers; she stayed safely behind her screens. It had always been enough for her to know how much she contributed to the effort, and the team had always made it clear they wouldn't have the record they had without her. But something about this made it different.

And that something was standing before her.

This was crazy. He'd just found out his murderer father was out of prison, and skulking around here at the ranch, but all he could seem to focus on was this woman, and finding out who the hell she really was, and how it stung to find out that she'd lied to him from the beginning.

Which was exactly yesterday.

How could it possibly matter so much that a woman he'd known less than twenty-four hours—and in fact had only spent about three hours with—had lied about who she was? What he should be focusing on was how the hell she knew about his father.

What you should be focusing on is if he's going to come after you for testifying against him. If he plans to kill you, too, like he killed Sarah.

He suppressed the burst of adrenaline that hit, the fight-or-flight urge.

"May I ask you something?"

Her voice was quiet, tentative. Yet he whirled on her as if she'd shouted. "Oh, sure, *Zoe.* You've only lied about who you are and won't tell me why you know what you know or even why you're here. So ask away."

He saw her wince, and quashed the jab of guilt he felt. She'd earned his anger, hadn't she? But she stood her ground, and didn't retaliate with a raised voice of her own when she asked, "Why is your father even eligible for parole so soon, after killing your girlfriend?"

He stared at her. He would have been stunned all over again, except he remembered she'd said she did research for some big company. And it wasn't like the story was some sort of secret, it had been all over the news back when it had happened. It was why she'd bothered to dig into this that mystified him. Or maybe that was suspicion gnawing at him, although he wasn't quite sure what he suspected her of, beyond lying.

When he finally spoke, he had to release his clenched jaw to do it. "He didn't 'kill' her. He murdered her. I don't care what that Montana 'mitigated deliberate homicide' law says, there was no heat of passion. He knew exactly what he was doing. He planned it out ahead of time. He even told me the plan, I was just too stupid to realize he actually meant it."

He hadn't vented that in a long time, and he wasn't sure why he'd done so now. *Three whole hours with her and you're spilling your guts? Even knowing she's a liar?*

"Why did he do it?" She said it as if she believed him, and that made him answer her.

"He hated her, he'd always hated her and he planned it out in advance. He even lured her to that place, at a time when he knew there'd be a lot of traffic heading to the big game at the high school."

"Why? Why did he hate her so much?"

"Because she called him what he was. A feckless loser." He closed his eyes for a moment. "She told him that after the way he'd treated me he had no right to the title 'father.' And that he should get out of my life and stay out."

"In other words," she said, her voice strangely soothing, "she stood up for you."

He opened his eyes and looked at her. There was a warmth in her eyes that startled him into saying, "In a way nobody ever had before. How could you know that?"

"I grew up a nerd, a geek, whatever you want to call it, before it was really cool, for girls anyway. Some people didn't get it." *Like me*, Kyle thought. *I hate the stuff.* "I got teased, harassed…until my three brothers banded together and made it clear the next person who made a jab at me would be dealing with them."

"That's great. I…never had that." He gave a bitter little laugh. "My half brother and I hate each other."

Zoe—or whatever her real name was—froze. But she didn't speak, so he finished the thought.

"Hard to believe half of it was over that…piece of cow manure. Our father didn't deserve even that much emotion from either of us."

She was staring at him now, and he had the feeling she was on the verge of saying something, but couldn't decide if she should. Which reminded him of what had started this whole conversation.

She was a liar. She was a liar, and he'd best remember that.

Chapter 14

There's your opening, go for it!

The words rang in Ashlynn's head, and she knew it was true, she might never get a better opening to probe about Xander. But she couldn't do it. Not now, not when she'd already had to admit she'd lied to him about who she was. Not when she'd dumped the horrible news of his father's release on him out of the blue. She could almost see her brothers shaking their heads at her, knew they'd have seized the opportunity and probably had all the information they needed in a matter of moments.

But she couldn't do it. She couldn't push him, not now, when he had this revelation to deal with. And perhaps a real threat, if it was indeed his father he'd seen, which seemed likely. And from what he'd told her, she had no trouble believing the man might well come after his own son for payback for daring to speak against him in court. Even if it hadn't worked.

She wondered why it hadn't. Why Kyle's testimony hadn't swayed them enough to go for a straight murder charge. She'd have to research that Montana law a little. But right now, she was stumbling for the right thing to say. For anything to say. Finally she settled on the most urgent thing.

"Do you think your father is here after you? For testifying against him?"

He laughed, but it was a short, harsh, brutal thing. "He's not here to say, 'Hello, son, I've missed you.' Only thing he's ever missed about me is having a handy punching bag."

"So you're in danger."

"He swore to me the day they carted him off to prison that I'd regret what I said in court. That I'd pay for it— he'd see to it."

She reached out instinctively and put a hand on his arm. "Kyle, you need to call the police, or the county sheriff, whoever handles law enforcement here. They need to know he's out, already here, and what he threatened."

"So you want me to call the law, the law who just let him out of prison and are so efficient they couldn't manage to call the one person with the most need to know?"

"That's the bureaucracy side, not the front line side. They're different."

She knew this to be true from first-hand personal experience; dealing with the people in the field and dealing with the administrative end of the FBI, the upper echelon, was like being in a firefight compared to walking through an endless maze full of fog and obfuscation.

She only realized that in her anxiousness over his safety she'd possibly said too much when his gaze sharp-ened and his eyes narrowed. "And just how," he said, "would you know that?"

She scrambled for cover. "The place I work does some business for the government. It's like that these days."

"You mean the people who do the work are good, but the people who tell them what work to do have their head up their—"

"Sort of, yes."

"I think I'll stick to ranch work. At least we've all got the same goal, taking care of the animals."

She sighed. "Sounds a lot more honest."

"Speaking of honesty…"

"I know, I know," she said, feeling awful that he knew she'd lied and was still keeping things from him. "But I can't."

"Orders from one of those higher-ups?"

"And my family."

That made him draw back and stare at her for a moment. Then he let out a long breath and the tension in the room seemed to ebb a bit.

"Please," she said, "make that call."

He shifted his gaze. Grimaced. Said nothing more. But he took out his phone and made the call.

To Kyle's surprise, he ended up speaking to the sheriff himself, a rather crusty guy named Frank Noonan. Apparently once he'd heard what it was about, he'd taken over the call.

"And you're sure you've seen him in the area?"

"Not just in the area. On the ranch."

"But he hasn't approached you yet?"

"No. Probably because I haven't been alone. He always did like the odds stacked in his favor."

"All right, son, listen. All my deputies will have the info and a photo, and they'll be looking for him. And I'll have the area deputy spend any slack time in your area. But we're stretched thin these days, and I can't afford to designate one-on-one personal security for you. You carrying?"

"I will be as soon as we hang up."

"Good."

"I don't suppose I can shoot him on sight?"

The sheriff laughed. "I wish. But no, don't get yourself into any trouble. He's not worth it."

That caught Kyle's curiosity. "No, he's not, but how do you know that?"

"I followed that trial, son. I saw you testify. He should have gone down for pure deliberate homicide. Sorry about your girl."

For a moment Kyle was speechless. Then, awkwardly, he said, "Thanks."

"Just so we're clear, you can't shoot him on sight, but if he threatens you, comes at you, you do what you need to do to protect yourself."

"I will." He was going to have to tell the Wesleys. He hoped they didn't fire him over bringing this down on the ranch. Hard to insure the safety of your guests if you had a killer hunting one of your employees.

"If you see him again, you call us right away. Try not to engage with him. Ideally, first contact should be us, so he knows we're watching him."

Not much in his life had happened in the ideal way so he didn't have much faith this would either, but he said only, "Yes, sir."

"In fact, take my number. Call me first, so I can get things going fast."

Startled, Kyle had to find something to write with since it wasn't the number he'd just called that he could save in his phone. "Got it," he said when he had it written down.

"Appreciate it if you don't spread that around."

"I'll bet," Kyle said, smiling for the first time since this had started.

After he'd hung up he stood there looking at the number he'd scrawled on the bag from the market where he'd picked up some food when he'd moved in here. And what Zoe—or whatever her name really was— had said went through his mind.

...the front line side. They're different.

"You're smiling."

She'd come up beside him, and the words were softly spoken, as if they—or his smile—made her happy. Telling himself not to wander any further down that path, since it had already gotten him in trouble, he didn't look at her as he input the number on his short contact list.

"He gave me his direct number. The sheriff himself."

"He did? That's…wow."

She sounded as impressed as he felt. And finally he looked at her. Into those warm, brown eyes. "He said he followed the trial. And that he believed me, that he'd planned it. That it shouldn't have come out the way it did."

She let out a breath that sounded relieved. "Then he's fully on your side. That's good, Kyle."

"Yeah." Then the reality of the situation hit anew. "He'll have his guys looking, but he doesn't have the manpower to have someone hanging around here all the time."

He put down the phone and walked over to the backpack that was sitting on the floor beside the single end table, mostly unpacked. He unzipped the largest side pocket and pulled out his older but well-maintained Smith & Wesson .38 revolver. He checked the load then slid it back into the holster and clipped it onto his belt. When he straightened, she was staring at him, her eyes wide with something akin to dread.

He'd lived his whole life in the free state of Montana, so it took him a moment. Then he grimaced. "Let me guess, you're a city girl who is terrified at the very sight of a weapon."

"Actually," she said, her voice chilly, "I grew up around them. My father was a cop. My brothers are also, of a sort. I'm not afraid of the tools they use, and I did my homework before I came to an open carry state. If I was upset, it was because this means you obviously believe your father is a threat, that he's come here to hurt you."

He stood there, feeling sorry he'd said it. But that was immediately overwhelmed by an odd sensation it took him a moment to recognize, he hadn't felt that kind of inner kick in so long.

Attraction.

No, he had to be wrong. It was just that he wasn't used to anybody caring if he got hurt. His father had always said he wasn't worth the worry, and his mother had been so worn down that when he turned eighteen he couldn't leave fast enough to suit her.

But here was this beautiful woman, worried about him. That was what had him off-balance. It had to be. Because the idea of anything more between this New York City visitor and a Montana cowboy was a dream that could only turn into a farce.

Chapter 15

Ashlynn sat in the desk chair, her arms wrapped around herself as she stared at the screen. She was sure most people would laugh at her, being here on a guest ranch dedicated to showing people the natural wonders of this admittedly beautiful place yet sitting here looking at her laptop instead of said place. But this was where she felt most comfortable, and she'd long ago accepted that fact.

And yet she felt the strangest urge to go back out to the barn and visit the horses. She realized most of them would probably be out—Kyle had said when he'd left they had to move some cattle, obviously on horseback—but maybe the young one he'd been working on would still be there. She'd like to see that pretty spotted coat again.

She grabbed up her jacket, hoping the temperature would be near the average she'd researched. As she stepped outside it struck her again how radically different a place this was. There was none of the noise she always took for granted, or the smells…or the afternoon crowds of people to dodge as she made her way to her destination. Here, the only thing she heard was the occasional whinny of a horse, the call of a bird from above—she'd swear that was an eagle or some sort of big raptor circling over there—and the air was crisp and clean, with none of the smells from street vendors, or the less pleasant exhaust odors or the stink of garbage that hadn't yet been picked up.

And no people.

When she got out far enough to look back through the windows of the main building, she could see movement in the big room where she'd checked in, but outside there was no one in sight. They'd told her October was nearing the start of their slow season, as snow began to arrive and visitors switched destinations to the local ski resorts. Although, the reception desk had told her, some of their regulars still came to the ranch and drove to the Bridger Bowl or other nearby ski spots. Ashlynn had thought it said a lot about this ranch that they inspired such loyalty.

But then, they had people like Kyle Slater working for them.

She remembered the review that had brought her here, and how he had helped a grieving little boy. As the story had then, the memory of it sparked a little burst of warmth inside her, amplified now that she'd met the man. She could so see it happening that way, could see him taking such care, just from watching his gentleness with the animals…especially this guy, she thought as she reached the stall of the young horse.

It was gratifying when the animal seemed to recognize her. At least, he greeted her with a soft nicker that made her smile.

"Hi, there," she said softly.

Hello, pretty boy.

Her own words echoed in her mind, along with the way she'd applied them to both males in this stall when she'd first seen them.

The colt came forward and stuck his head over the closed bottom of the stall door. Slowly—did horses bite?—she held out her hand. When the animal snuffled at it, she risked stroking his nose. It was softer than she would have imagined, and he didn't seem to mind at all.

"Your friend Kyle getting you used to being touched, huh?"

A little snort, as if he recognized the name, startled her and she almost jumped. Or maybe it was just that her brain had put together Kyle and being touched. That sensation that had rippled through her when he'd helped her down from Daisy made a reappearance simply at the thought.

He didn't seem to mind as she reached further, stroking his head, and finally his neck. In fact he seemed to enjoy it, although she did wonder if perhaps he might be expecting a treat of some kind. She should have asked about that. Horses liked apples, didn't they? And sugar cubes? She supposed it was a measure of how distracted Kyle made her that she hadn't even thought of it. She'd have to remember that for next time.

Next time.

Already she was planning a next time. She almost laughed at herself.

She gave the spotted horse a final pat and began walking down the rows of stalls, stopping at each one that held an animal to look. Daisy, she noticed, was gone, and she wondered if there was another rank beginner here who was out for a lesson. Somehow her earlier connection with the horse spiked her curiosity, and she opened the lower half of the Dutch-style door. Cautiously, first checking the straw on the floor of the stall with the idea of dodging any droppings, she stepped into the stall.

It was roomier than she'd realized, but it had to be she supposed for an animal that likely was nearly ten times her weight. The straw seemed clean, and there was a bit of hay in a net hanging from the wall that lent a fresh scent. All in all, a fairly pleasant place to be. As long as you got out now and then, as Daisy obviously did. Now she herself, give her a computer and access, and she could go for days without setting foot outside.

Then again, she had to admit that outside here in the country was a very different thing. Maybe it was just the strangeness, the newness, to her at least, but she was finding it surprisingly appealing.

She looked around, realizing that this stall had solid walls that only went as high as the half door and were screened above that, unlike others where the wall went up to the rafters. She wondered if, like people, there were horses that liked to be around other horses, and those that didn't. If there were extrovert horses and introvert horses. If that applied to how they felt about people, too. And if—

Her phone signaled an incoming text with the tone she'd assigned to the team messages. She yanked it out of her jacket pocket. Dropped it, freaked, then realized the hit had been cushioned by the straw. She bent to pick the phone up, brushed off the fragments of straw that clung to it, then laughed out loud at doing something she never would have imagined, clearing her cell phone's screen of bedding from a horse's stall.

The text was from Patrick. And reality slammed into her. She'd been so sucked into the drama here—and meeting Kyle and dealing with her uncharacteristic response to him—that she'd pushed what she was really here for to the back of her mind.

And hadn't really reconciled, in her heart anyway, the fact that Kyle was Xander's half brother.

She made herself open the text and read.

We're going over what evidence we have from all the crime scenes millimeter by millimeter, trying to match your suspect's DNA or prints, even partially. She knew they had both on file for Xander, as an FBI employee. So far, nothing. He's either very, very careful, or not our guy. We'll keep at it.

She hesitated, still finding even the possibility hard to believe, but in the end she knew she had to do it. So she tapped in an answer.

He's smart enough to be very, very careful. And I've learned something here that's probably nothing but is interesting. It appears my suspect's biological father is a killer.

A moment passed before Patrick answered. Details?! She gave him the bones of the story.

You get this from the half brother?

The half brother. Funny how the very term she'd used herself seemed so cold, unfeeling, and wrong now that she'd met the man.

Not at first. It was news here. Victim was his girlfriend. He testified against his father.

Straight arrow, then?

I think so.

She hovered over the screen, undecided whether to mention that said father was now out of prison and probably hunting down said half brother. In the end she decided no, because there was nothing Patrick or any of them could do from there, and they needed to be there working on the Landmark Killer case. So instead she tapped out and sent a rather vague message.

Things a little more complicated here than expected. Might take a while to work out.

Problem?

Nothing I can't deal with. Yet, she added silently.

She just had to hope it stayed that way.

"Hey."

She nearly dropped the phone into the straw again. She spun around, to see Kyle leaning with his elbows on the bottom half of the stall door, looking at her. He hadn't, she noticed, used her name.

Her fake name.

"Hi," she said, and it sounded a little too bright even to her.

He nodded at the stall she was standing in. "Checking out the accommodations?"

She managed a smile a little better than her greeting. "I guess I was. It seems nice. Roomy, clean."

"We see to that. Shoveling sh—horse manure is part of the cost of getting to be this close to them."

He said it as if it were a privilege, and she found she liked that he thought of it that way.

Oh, good, something else to like about him.

Xander's half brother.

She thought of all the lunches they'd shared, she and Xander. All the friendly conversations about movies or the latest tech trend. In all that time she'd felt not even a spark of anything more.

Not even a trace of what she was feeling now.

Chapter 16

She was looking at him so intently Kyle wondered if he'd missed a spot shaving, or unknowingly smeared dirt on his face. Finally, because he was starting to feel a bit unnerved, by her stare and his own reaction to it, he straightened up from leaning on the stall door. But instead of taking the easy way out, claiming work to do and walking away, he blurted out something he hadn't planned to do until this moment.

"I was going to let Splash out for a run in the corral. You know, if you want to come along. He's kind of fun to watch when he's loose."

"I'd love to," she said, and there was no denying the enthusiasm was genuine. He suspected she'd kind of fallen for the striking young horse. Which was understandable. The colt's flash and personality—in her case coupled with the simple fact that he seemed to like her when he liked few—was darn near irresistible. Of course, the other hands might argue that; they hadn't spent as much time with Splash, and it seemed the youngster had noticed and wasn't quite as cooperative with them.

She came out of Daisy's stall, and closed the door behind her, asking as she did, "She's all right? Her leg I mean?"

"Fine," he said. "She's working today."

"Nursing another novice?"

He smiled at her words, and how honestly she said them. "No, actual ranch work. We try to vary things, so the horses don't get burned-out doing the same thing every day."

She smiled back at him as they walked the barn's aisle. "You sound happy with the way they do things here."

He shrugged. "I am. I mean, it's a business like any other ranch, and a lot of hard-core hands think working for a guest ranch is selling out, but I like the Wesleys, and like you said, the way they do things. They know the horses are the heart of this place, and they treat them accordingly."

"How long have you been here?"

"Coming up on a year," he said, feeling a sudden, unexpected jab of edginess. He wasn't used to feeling that way at the mere thought of doing what he'd done so many times before, moving on. He'd always thought he would continue his nomadic life forever, until one day he made a wrong step and wound up falling off a mountain or got too up close and personal with a rattlesnake or something.

"Maybe you should—" She cut herself off.

"Maybe I should what?"

"Nothing." She sounded a little tense. "It's none of my business.

They were at Splash's stall now, so he let it slide. The colt greeted him happily, and when he asked if he wanted to play, the horse gave an undeniably enthusiastic snort.

"Do horses understand a lot of words, like dogs do?" she asked.

He liked that she wanted to know. "I'm no expert scientifically, but they understand a few. They're more about visual reaction, I think. And combined cues, like a word and a nudge." He smiled at her. "So they're not just big dogs, if that's what you mean."

She laughed at that. "No, I was just wondering how different they are."

"Just remember, dogs are essentially predators. Horses are prey, and they know it and act accordingly. They cooperate with us once they trust us, but they're always ready to spook and run because they have to be."

She was staring at him again. "I…never would have thought about it that way."

He shrugged. "No reason you should. And this guy—" he reached out and slapped Splash's neck "—can put on a pretty good dog act." The young horse snorted again and head-butted his hand, as if to urge him to hurry up. Kyle glanced at the woman beside him, found her smiling widely, and added, "I rest my case."

He grabbed the halter that hung beside the stall door and slipped it over the colt's head. He led him out of the stall and they walked side by side, the three of them, with him in the middle.

Not bad, Slater. Great colt on one side, sexy lady on the other. Enjoy it, it won't last.

When they got outside Splash's head came up as he excitedly looked around. The energetic colt danced sideways a little now and then, out of pure excitement. Kyle noticed Zoe—or whoever she really was—looked at the horse when he did. Aware, but not afraid. And probably why she'd picked the spot with him between her and the horse. A good place for a newb to be.

When they reached the big turnout corral, he held the lead with one hand as he unlatched the gate. Splash was skipping a bit constantly now, clearly knowing that in a moment he would be free to run, roll and generally frolic.

"He's excited," he explained when he saw that her glance looked a bit more concerned. "He knows he gets cut loose once we're inside."

"What should I do?" she asked. Then, with a wry smile, added, "Or not do?"

He couldn't seem to help it, he smiled back at her. He still had no idea who she really was, even her real name, but here he was smiling at her like a moonstruck calf.

"Probably not go in with him to dance, at least not just yet. You could sit on the fence though, if you want. Or just watch from outside."

She nodded, then turned and grabbed the top rail of the fence. She climbed up easily enough, swung her feet around and settled in. He turned his attention back to Splash, who was now dancing like a parade horse. He double-checked the gate, then reached up to unfasten the buckle of the halter.

When it fell away, the young horse stood there quivering, staring at Kyle. He waited five seconds, so far the limit of the colt's patience, before slapping his neck. "Go for it," he said.

The little Appy spun around on his hind feet and took off in a head-bouncing, heel-kicking romp. He let out a delighted whinny about two steps in, and Kyle heard whoever-she-was laugh. He didn't like that it still stung that she'd lied to him, but it did.

It's for my own safety. My family insisted.

Her words came back to him. Okay, maybe he should cut her some slack. If she really was in danger, then she had the right to do whatever it took to stay safe.

Like Sarah wouldn't?

She had refused to believe his father could be lethal, and had stood up to him at every turn. Most of the time for his sake. And in the end, it had cost her her life. And Kyle knew he would feel responsible for that for the rest of his.

He heard…okay, Zoe, for now, laugh as she watched Splash cavort. He climbed up beside her on the top rail just as Splash dropped to the ground for a roll and she laughed again.

"Why do they like that, rolling in the dirt like that?"

"Probably the back-scratching effect," he answered.

"Oh. I get that completely, then. Nothing worse than an itch you can't scratch."

Telling himself sternly there had been absolutely no innuendo in that, he merely let out an assenting, "Mmm."

Splash was up again, trotting around the corral like a show horse now. There was silence as they watched for a long moment before she broke it.

"Are you all right? You looked awfully serious there for a moment."

So she hadn't missed that moment when he'd thought of Sarah.

"Have you seen him again?" Her soft voice held obvious concern. "Your father?"

"I...no. Not today. But then I wasn't here since this morning, until now."

"So you don't think he's...like roaming the ranch?"

"No sign of anyone, or any unknown vehicles. And he wouldn't be riding, he hates horses."

"Well, that right there tells you he's not to be trusted," she said, sounding like she meant it, which made him smile. "So how did you end up loving them?"

"I got a part-time job working at a ranch fairly close to home while I was in school." A wry grimace twisted his mouth. "We needed the money anyway, but at least my mother let me work there instead of someplace in town that might have paid more."

"How old were you?"

"Twelve."

She blinked. "That's...young."

"That's why they paid me in cash," he admitted. "Not much, a few bucks a day, but it kept me in lunch money for school, and my mother was glad she didn't have to do it. Not that she would have." She stared at him for a long moment. Silently. "Something wrong?" he finally asked, an edge creeping into his voice. He'd grown up used to some people looking down on him for their poor circumstances. Somehow he hadn't expected it from her.

"Yes," she answered, surprising him further. Then she disarmed him completely by adding, "What's wrong is me taking for granted how good I had it as a kid. Before my dad...died, anyway."

He wondered if that moment's hesitation was because it was still painful, or something else.

"Is your mom still alive?"

"Yes. She had a hard time raising four kids alone, but did her best. She's living in Florida now, and is much happier there."

Four kids? And his mother had barely hung on with one. Apparently he'd misjudged this—and her—entirely, thinking she was a spoiled city girl who'd never hit a rough spot in her life.

Until maybe now. When whatever was going on made her lie about who she was.

Chapter 17

She'd nearly blown it.

In her head, Ashlynn was still hearing her response to when he'd told her he'd been here almost a year. *Maybe you should stay this time.* Which of course would have betrayed that she knew about his habit of usually moving on every year. Which would tell him she'd done much more than just stumbled across the information about his father; she had dug it up. Small difference to some, but she had a definite feeling he was not one of those.

She wondered, not for the first time, how her brothers who were field agents managed to do any undercover work at all without blowing it.

They're trained agents. You're a geek. And never the twain shall entwine. Or something.

She was glad of the distraction of watching Splash run and play, because it seemed the less she talked to or even looked at Kyle Slater, the better off she was. There was something about the man that made her lose her focus, in a way she never, ever did.

And made her say stupid things about itches you can't scratch.

Splash finally trotted back over to them, let out a little whinny as he nudged Kyle's knee. Ashlynn watched him drop down from the fence with easy grace, and pat the gleaming black neck. He grabbed the halter from where he'd hung it over a fence post and slipped it back over the young horse's head. Then he looked back up at her. Started to speak and then hesitated, giving her the silly idea he was as hyper-aware of her as she was of him.

"Fun part's over," he said after a moment. "Time for some pretty routine work with him now, so you might want to take off and find something more interesting to do."

More interesting? Than watching you?

"I'd like to watch him in class, too." She gave him a smile she hoped didn't betray her wayward thoughts. "If the professor doesn't mind, of course."

He let out a short, sharp laugh. "First and last time I'll be called that," he said. "But stay if you want. It might even help, because he needs to learn to focus."

"He does?"

"He's a little…distractible. Not great for a ranch horse. It annoys my boss, and I know he's thinking he's not worth it."

"Oh, no," she exclaimed, surprised at how much that stung. How could anyone not like the beautiful, sassy little horse? "He wouldn't get rid of him, would he?"

"Might, if I can't disprove that old saying about white feet."

She blinked. What on earth? "White feet?"

"It's an old superstition, but it seems to live on in some quarters."

"About a horse with white feet?" she asked, looking down at Splash's four indeed white hooves, and the also white markings above them, that she thought were just called socks. Or maybe stockings. It fit.

"Yep," Kyle said. "They—that big, anonymous 'they,' say 'One white foot, buy him. Two white feet, try him. Three white feet, look well about him. Four white feet, go without him.'"

"Well, that's silly. He's beautiful, and so are his feet!"

"Doesn't matter how pretty he is if he's a spook fest. Especially here, where he has to be safe around greenhorns—" He cut himself off and looked away. "Oops. Sorry."

Ashlynn laughed, the most genuinely amused laugh she'd let out in a while. He was so sweet! "What are you apologizing for? I am a greenhorn, and I know it. That's why I want to watch and learn."

He looked back at her again. He tilted his head slightly, in a way that she found oddly endearing. *Lord, you're sliding down that slope fast...*

"Are you like that about everything? Wanting to learn, I mean?"

"I like to learn new things. And the more I like something, the more I want to learn about it."

The more I like something indeed. She groaned inwardly at the double layer in her own words, but with an effort kept a straight face.

And so she stayed seated on the top rail of the fence,

watching him work with Splash. And she saw what he meant, the young horse seemed quite distracted by her presence. He kept looking her way while Kyle was trying to get him to focus on various moves on the lead, staying close, moving around him in a circle, changing direction. Sort of like training a dog to the leash, she imagined.

But what she noticed most of all was Kyle's patience. He never lost his temper or changed his tone or his own movements, just began again each time. And she remembered what he'd said earlier. *Horses are prey, and they know it and act accordingly. They cooperate with us once they trust us, but they're always ready to spook and run because they have to be.*

When Splash finally seemed to have settled into the walks in the center of the big corral, Kyle shifted to circling the perimeter. And it began again, every time they got close to her the colt would start to dance around. And again Kyle stayed calm, patient and gentle.

She had never realized how much work went into training a horse in such a basic thing. Or maybe it was just this horse. Maybe this skittishness went with the flashy coloring. She'd have to look into that. Do a little research on Appaloosas and their characteristics.

Are you like that about everything?

...the more I like something, the more I want to learn about it.

It was the truth. And she liked this horse with the vivid coloring to match his slightly chaotic personality. But she liked Daisy, with her calm, sweet nature, too. She was finding she liked horses in general. She was here on a ranch, after all, wasn't that to be expected?

As for the man being so patient with this particular horse…that was much, much trickier ground.

Splash was coming along. The horse had finally gotten to the point where he stopped the head-tossing dance every time they got close to where she was sitting on the fence, and merely turned his head slightly to look at her when they passed. Kyle figured that was progress enough for one day. Especially since he himself had a particular reaction every time they got close to her. Whether she was watching intently or smiling in encouragement didn't seem to matter, his gut still clenched into that little knot and his pulse kicked up.

All the times you've shaken your head over the guys who fell for visitors, and here you are, circling the drain yourself. About a woman you met exactly yesterday?

He called himself a few choice names and made himself concentrate on Splash. He really was worried that, while he'd given him license to regularly work with the colt, Matt might finally decide the colt was too much trouble, that he would never settle down the way he needed to to be a part of the program here. Kyle saw his point, they couldn't afford to have a horse that might be dangerous to a novice rider when a large part of their clientele was just that. And since Splash was only two years old, Matt or his father might run out of patience before the young horse settled down, if he ever did. He'd nearly been there when Kyle had asked for a chance at settling the skittish animal down. He'd agreed, but made it pretty clear he was the colt's last shot.

Kyle felt an odd pang. When he left, which would be soon—especially now, with his crazy father on the loose—who would take over working with Splash?

Would anyone care enough to go slow with him, to give him the time needed to convince him that humans—most of them, anyway—weren't the predators he needed to worry about? Would anyone be willing to spend the extra hours it would take? Most of the hands wanted their off time to themselves, but they had friends and family around. He didn't.

No? You've got your old man around, Slater.

His jaw tightened at the thought. Splash snorted and tried to turn to face him, as if he'd sensed the sudden shift. Or maybe it was just because they were nearing that spot on the fence where "Zoe"—he mentally added the quotation marks around the fake name—was sitting.

Maybe it was the mental juxtaposition of her with that thought about his father, but suddenly what she'd told him hit him in a different sort of way. At the time she'd admitted to using a false name, he'd just been hit with the news his father was loose, and he'd been pretty fixated on that. But now what she'd said rang differently in his head.

It's for my own safety.

Maybe she had someone in her life like his old man. Someone brutal, evil. Maybe that's who she was here hiding from. And maybe he should think about that instead of focusing so solely and self-centeredly on his own troubles.

The jab of guilt he felt made him smile a little more widely at her as they passed. A little more welcoming. Her eyes widened slightly, but she smiled back at him. The guilt faded away, to be replaced by something entirely different.

If she needs to be Zoe, let her be Zoe.

When they finally headed back to the barn, Splash

reached out and nudged her arm with his nose, almost affectionately. She laughed delightedly.

"He definitely likes you," Kyle said, unable to stop his own grin at that note of gratification in her voice.

And it's not just the horse...

He tried to shake it off, telling himself he had better get himself back in line. He had no business getting involved with a guest. True, it was almost time for him to move on, but he didn't want to do it under a cloud, or because he was fired.

"Would he let me brush him, do you think?"

There was such eagerness in her voice it made him smile all over again. "I think he would."

"But you'll stay close, just in case?"

Not nearly as close as I'd like to.

He clamped down on it again, that unexpected rush of attraction. He hadn't had a reaction like this to...well, anyone. Not even Sarah. He might be only six years older than he'd been when they'd first found each other, but it felt like a couple of decades. Having your own father murder your girlfriend would do that to a guy.

Now that he could look back more rationally, he suspected that had been as much youth and rampaging hormones as anything, multiplied by Sarah's utter fearlessness. The fearlessness—especially when standing up to his father—that had gotten her killed in the end.

Splash indeed tolerated her efforts. Kyle kept his interference to a minimum, telling her only that she could brush harder, and that when it came to his hind feet and tail to let him handle it, since the colt could get a little lively then.

He was working on one of those feet when something

caught his eye. He released the hoof, hanging onto the hoof pick as he straightened up.

"You'd better get up to the dining room or you'll miss dinner," he said rather abruptly.

Her brow furrowed, probably at the edge that had come into his voice.

"But I should finish him, shouldn't I?"

"He's done enough. Go eat."

She was clearly puzzled, and it echoed in her voice. "Why don't you come with me, and eat too? You must be starved after working all day."

He could tell by the uncertainty in her tone that she'd had to work up to saying that. And the thought of spending a leisurely hour or so at a table with her was beyond tempting. But he knew what his answer had to be, for more than one reason.

"That would be inappropriate, Ms. Lamont," he said formally.

She drew back sharply. And without another word she turned and left. But not, he noticed, without giving Splash a goodbye pat.

He watched her go, then nudged the horse into his stall. He unhooked the lead line, leaving the halter on the colt for now, and backed out of the stall. He secured the door with his left hand, adjusting the position of the hoof pick in his right. It wasn't much of a weapon, but it was all he had at hand at the moment since his .38 was in the tack room instead of where it should be, on his belt.

So it was uncomfortable. As uncomfortable as dying, idiot?

That pick would leave a mark, if there was enough push behind it, but who knew what he was up against.

He was an idiot; he should have been carrying his .38 every minute after he'd hung up from that phone call from the prison. It wasn't a powerhouse .45 Semi-Auto, but it would do the job at this range.

But he didn't have it. So now he had to deal. He turned around to face the back door of the barn. And when he spoke he kept his tone bored and dismissive.

"Nice of you to drop in, *Dad*."

Chapter 18

It had been like flipping a switch, Ashlynn thought. One minute they'd been joking and acting like friends, the next he was all formal and distant.

At first she'd thought it was her perhaps thoughtless suggestion he join her for dinner. She should have realized there were rules, no doubt, about associating with the customers. And if it had been only that, she would have understood, and felt bad for putting him in the position where he had to say no and remind her of the difference between them.

Maybe she should count it as a good reminder that he worked here, and therefore had to be nice to her. And if she built it up into anything more in her silly mind, it was her own fault if she got her feelings hurt.

She felt uncertain enough that she ordered her evening meal to her cabin. The only other guests here now were a family with two children and an obviously tight clique of four women who gave off the same vibe of the clique that had tormented her for her geekiness in high school. She was in no state of mind to deal with either group just now.

Besides, she needed to check in, both to let the team know she was fine, and find out if they'd made any progress. Then she'd dive into her online space, following trails, scrambling down rabbit holes, doing anything but thinking about the guy who'd thrown her mind into such chaos.

But first she needed to warm up this room. She checked her weather app and saw it was supposed to get down to freezing tonight. Something that didn't usually happen for at least another couple of months back home in the city.

At least it's not their record of ten below.

She shivered at the thought, and went to turn on the gas fireplace. She stood there watching as it leaped to life at the turn of a knob, wondering if a wood fire would be not warmer, but more pleasant. Not that she would have the slightest idea how to build one. No, as close as she came to that was using a fire emoji in a text or email.

She'd never thought of her life, her world, as…limited. How could she, living in one of the biggest cities and centers of activity in the world? Yet coming here, seeing the vast expanse of this country, the mountains that were nearly twice as tall as any back in New York—and they weren't anywhere near the tallest ones in the state—the vast open spaces, the sheer expanse of it all made her feel smaller than even the towering skyscrapers she was used to.

She thought of the drive out here from her hotel in town, thought of what they'd passed along the way, or rather, what they hadn't passed. No wonder people here laughed at the idea of doing without their cars and trucks. In the city you could find pretty much anything within walking distance or hail a cab with a simple wave of a hand. Here, not so much. It was an entirely different way of life, and one she wasn't sure she could handle despite the surprising fact that it appealed to her.

And who would have ever expected that? Her brothers would hurt themselves laughing at the idea of her, born and bred city girl, liking this time spent in the wide open spaces.

And it has nothing to do with a certain cowboy who makes your heart skip a beat and then race to catch up...

She let out a long, sighing breath. She'd spent more time in introspection in the short time she'd been here than she had since she was a floundering teenager, uncertain of the world and her place in it.

So she dived back into that online world she knew so well, trying to shove out of her mind this new world that had her so off-balance. And the images of that cowboy being so patient and gentle with a flashy young black and white horse.

"I'd say thanks for all the visits, but you didn't make any, did you?"

The old man's voice was the same, raspy, a touch bitter with a dash of whine. The rasp from a lifetime of cigarettes, like the one he was pulling out now, the bitterness from a foiled sense of entitlement, and the whine because life hadn't turned out the way he thought he deserved. Kyle knew all that, because Sarah had helped him see it.

Sarah, who had stood up for him in a way he never had for himself. Sarah, who had taught him how to do it.

There was nothing else he could do for her now, except to not forget what he'd learned from her. And so his voice was cool, unrattled and leavened with the one thing he knew for certain would get to the old man. Amusement.

"I made," he said with a crooked smile, "the exact number of trips you're worth."

He saw it hit home. Saw the flush rising up his father's neck. "If you think I'm going to forget how you turned on me, you stinking little traitor, you've got another think coming."

"By 'turn on you' you mean telling the truth? That you're a vicious, cold-blooded killer who murdered Sarah? Yeah, I did that. Sorry, not sorry."

The flush had reached his face. "You stinking bastard—"

"I'm sure you'd be happier if I was. Regret marrying her, Mr. Hit-and-Run? Happier fathering kids on any woman you could trick into thinking you were human?"

The swearing got worse, a tirade of words that would even make the toughest of the ranch hands raise an eyebrow. But then the man he hated to admit was his father said words that changed everything.

"I've seen you with that sexy little brunette. How sweet."

It took a serious effort to keep his voice level, casual. "She's a guest at the ranch. I have to be nice."

"Looked more than just being nice to me. So tell me, is she as mouthy as the last one?"

"You'll never know, because you'll never get within

three feet of her," he snapped. The instant he did he regretted what he'd betrayed.

"Well, well," Victor said. "Looks like I found the right button to push. You just don't learn, do you? You always did have that Galahad complex. Which is good for me. Because after what you took from me, you think I'm going to let you just live and be happy?

"What *I* took from *you*?" Kyle stared at his father incredulously.

"I spent all that time in that hellhole of a prison because of you—"

"You murdered Sarah! It should have been the rest of your rotten life."

His father smiled, and it wasn't a nice one. "And instead, I'll spend the rest of that life making sure you spend yours alone. Starting with the new one. Zoe, right?"

He knew her name. He'd been watching them closely enough that he knew her name. It didn't matter just now that it wasn't her real name, because his father was here now and an alias wouldn't save her. Not from this man.

A chill went through him. Followed by a rush of panicked thoughts. He'd stayed here too long. He'd let down his guard. He'd trusted the system. He'd assumed Victor was safely locked away.

He'd done this to her, just as he had to Sarah.

His father laughed. That gleefully wicked sort of laugh he'd hoped never to hear again. The one he heard in his nightmares.

A sudden fierceness seized him. It was all he could do not to cross the six feet between them and bury the hoof pick in his face. "If you so much as look at her sideways, I won't testify against you this time. Because you won't be alive for a trial."

For a moment his father looked startled, like someone who'd thought he was dealing with a docile puppy but suddenly found himself cornered by a snarling, angry wolf. Kyle took a certain pleasure in that.

"You wouldn't dare—"

Victor cut himself off as his gaze shifted, looking past Kyle, toward the other end of the barn. Instantly he dodged back out the barn door, out of sight. Kyle spun around to see Matt coming in the other end of the barn. He had his phone to his ear, and was checking the stalls as he walked, so Kyle guessed he hadn't seen the old man. Which left him in a dilemma. Just how much should he tell his boss?

Run. Just get out of here. You were going to leave soon anyway. So run, and make sure the old man knows you're gone, so it won't accomplish anything for him to go after her.

He knew the moment he thought it that there was a huge hole in his gut-reaction thoughts. Because there was absolutely no guarantee that his father wouldn't go after her anyway, just because he was who and what he was, a cold, heartless brute.

Besides, he was tired of running. More tired of it than he had ever realized until now. He liked this place, and had gotten a sort of enjoyment he'd never expected out of introducing greenhorns to the life he loved. Sure, there were some cranky ones, but there were that kind of people everywhere. Most of them were nice enough, some of them really nice.

And then there was Zoe.

It hit him then, full force. What he had to do, and what he could not do.

He couldn't run. Not and take the chance his father

would leave her alone. Whatever problem had brought her here, the last thing she needed was to have run smack into his own disaster. But she had. Simply by being nice to him she'd put a target on her own back. And he'd made his father zero in by letting it happen, by even enjoying the rare connection he'd felt, by indulging in the mild flirting. All because he'd known she'd be gone soon.

And now she couldn't be gone soon enough, because Victor Slater was already here and had her in his sights.

It was up to him to make sure she didn't wind up as Sarah had.

Ashlynn only realized she hadn't blinked in a while when the knock on her cabin door snapped her out of her concentration on the screen. She was going to need the eye drops her doctor had recommended soon. She tried to remind herself, but she got so deep into her work sometimes—

The knock came again, sharper, harder this time, sounding rather urgent. And a voice.

"Zoe?"

Kyle. It was Kyle. She jumped to her feet.

"Zoe, it's Kyle, please open the door."

He sounded as urgent as that knock had been. Was he hurt? Had his father shown up? Her thoughts raced and her stomach roiled a little as she ran over to the door and pulled it open.

"What's wrong? Are you all right?" she asked anxiously.

"No," he answered, his expression as grim as his tone as he stepped inside. He immediately pushed the door shut behind him, then leaned against it as if to hold the outside out. It was then that she realized, with a little jolt of shock, that he was wearing that gun she'd seen earlier on his hip.

She knew—she was nothing if not thorough—that Montana was the freest state for gun owners, when it came to laws restricting them. And she'd seen them in plain view since she'd come here, something her city born and bred mind had had to adjust to. But right now the presence of that weapon on this man could mean only one thing.

"Your father?" she guessed, and read the answer in the way his jaw tightened.

"He's here."

Immediately the pieces fell together in her mind. "That's what you saw. Out in the barn. Why you went all stiff and formal."

"For all the good it did." He sounded almost bitter now.

"Kyle—"

"I was trying to divert him, show him that you weren't...what he thought. But he's been watching. Watching...us."

"Us, together?" she asked.

He nodded. "And he thinks we're..."

His voice trailed off just as realization struck, that her attraction to him must have been obvious. But why would that matter to his father—

Her breath caught. *His father murdered his girl-friend.* "You think he thinks we're...together, so he'll come after me?"

"He's already promised he will. And I'm not making the same mistake I made before, not taking him seriously. I didn't believe he'd do it when he threatened

Sarah, and she died because of it. I'm not letting the same thing happen to you. Pack up your stuff."

She drew back. "What?"

"Get everything you need together. You're getting out of here, this place is too vulnerable."

"What, you're evicting me? Kyle, I can't just go back home." The absurdity of this new development struck her hard. "There's a killer looking for me there, too."

Kyle's brows rose as his eyes widened. "What?"

"It's a long story—"

"That we don't have time for. Get ready to move."

"Move where?"

His mouth twisted into a grimace. "We're heading for the hills."

Chapter 19

Kyle was a little amazed at how…cooperative she'd been. She'd merely studied him for a few seconds, then turned around and begun to do what he'd asked. She picked up a backpack—a much newer, sleeker thing than his, and one he would guess had never seen anything other than tech and maybe a water bottle and snacks—and began to gather her things.

Most of which, he'd noticed, seemed to be electronic gadgets. A laptop and a cell phone—at least he thought it was a cell phone, although it looked like some wild cross between a smart phone and a walkie talkie—those he recognized, but the other stuff, the things the gadgets were plugged into, and what was plugged into them, was beyond him. Sometimes he wondered if his dislike of the stuff wasn't completely because of his brother's love for it, but because he knew it was likely beyond him.

"You really need all that?" he asked.

She looked at him as if he'd suggested she leave a finger or two behind. "Of course I do."

"There's no internet where we're going," he warned.

She nodded toward the array of gear she'd started to slip into a case with foam slots that looked custom cut to fit the various pieces. "There will be."

He gave a shake of his head before he got too deep into things he didn't understand, and focused on the one thing he did; he needed to get her away from here, and out of his father's reach.

She headed for the small closet, then stopped and looked back at him, her expression more worried than it had been. "How are we getting to this place?"

"Don't panic. We're driving." Although he would rather have ridden, if only because his father couldn't, he'd then have a horse to worry about feeding and caring for. Not to mention asking a woman who'd been aboard a horse exactly once to take a ride that long and over some rough ground, was out of the question. "My boss is letting me borrow one of the ranch trucks."

Her eyes widened. "Your boss? I didn't think—what about your job, your work?"

"He's a good guy. And luckily we're slow right now." *And unlucky, since it gives my father fewer obstacles.*

"So…he knows?"

His jaw tightened as he remembered how humiliating it had been to have to explain to the man he respected what a mess his life was.

"I never lied to him," he said quickly, not sure why he felt so compelled to explain. "He's always known my father was in prison, and why."

"But now he knows he's out and…"

"Looking to kill again. Yes."

She started moving more quickly now, as if the reality had sunk in. She rolled rather than folded clothes and tucked them into the relatively small, compared to many guests' anyway, suitcase. She disappeared into the bathroom and came out moments later with a zippered bag she also put in the case. She hurried over to the nightstand beside the bed—the bed he was carefully not looking at, since he was trying not to think of her in it—and picked up yet another device, something he guessed was an e-reader of some kind. That went in a side pocket of what he guessed served her as a purse, lying on the bed next to the suitcase.

She closed up all three pieces, suitcase, briefcase and purse, then straightened to look at him. "Do I need to… tell anyone? The desk or—"

"No. My boss is letting everyone know."

"Your boss is being very helpful."

He sucked in a deep, pained breath, and closed his eyes for a moment. Then, steadier now, he opened his eyes to meet her troubled gaze. "They're good people, the family that own and run this place. The best."

They were, and he'd brought this down on them as well. *Let this be the final time you have to learn this lesson. You can't have this. You've been a loner for a reason, and you have to stay that way.*

He knew it was true. He couldn't even toy with the idea of staying, as he had been doing. It didn't matter how much he liked it here, he couldn't stay. And the fact that this woman stirred him to other thoughts he didn't dare indulge in only underlined the grim truth of his life.

That he was about to commit to spending an unknown length of time with her, hunkering down in a small, isolated cabin, didn't, couldn't be allowed to change that. He wouldn't be able to keep a lot of physical space between them in such confined quarters, so he would have to shore up the mental boundaries. Because underneath this all, the bedrock that was unyielding, was that any woman who dared to care about him could end up dead.

Telling himself he was being too full of himself to think Zoe cared about him in that way—in any way, really—he clamped down on the emotions he'd never had so much trouble with before.

"Put that on," he said as she grabbed the last thing from the closet, a puffy-style coat about the color of her dark brown hair, that looked as if it would hit her midthigh—*Stop it, Slater!* "It'll be colder up where we're going."

She did, then grabbed that shiny mass of hair and pulled it free of the collar. She didn't protest when he picked up the suitcase, but when he reached for the hard-sided case on the desk she shook her head and grabbed it first. "I've got it."

She said it possessively, in the tone of someone who didn't want it out of her sight. And then he put the suitcase in the back seat of the truck, next to his own backpack and small duffle, taking care to secure it so it didn't slide and crush the couple of bags of food that sat atop the ice chest on the floor. The resident chef had been more than generous, although Kyle suspected that had been at Matt's orders. Kyle wasn't sure why he was being so helpful, and hoped he'd have the chance to find out someday.

When he asked if she wanted her briefcase in the

back too, she firmly said no. She also gave the rifle in the rack in the back window of the truck's cab a wary glance. He wondered what she'd say when she saw the multiple ammo cans that were stashed under the seat. Then he reminded himself she wasn't a stranger to guns, even if she wasn't comfortable with them herself.

She climbed into the truck with that touch of awkwardness that told him she wasn't used to vehicles that sat this high, slid the case down to the floor at her feet, and reached for the seat belt.

As he walked around to the driver's side, he tried to understand the protectiveness. Valuable equipment, he supposed. Or maybe it wasn't hers, maybe it was from work and she was responsible for it. That made more sense to him. He might not know what all the widgets and gadgets were, but he had no doubt they were expensive because it all seemed to be.

Either that, or she was just one of those who lived and died online. That made him grimace slightly, but he made sure it was gone before he climbed in beside her. After all, who the hell was he to critique how anyone else lived their life? It was his father they were running from.

There's a killer looking for me there, too.

Her words slammed back into him. They were in for a bit of a drive, so he might as well ask. But before he could, she spoke.

"You've been to…where we're going?"

"Yes." He could almost feel her looking at him, so he tried to think of something else to say about it. "It's kind of like my place. A lot bigger, though. More updated. It's empty now because they don't rent it out that often."

"Why? What's wrong with it?"

"Too remote for most people. Last person who rented it was a writer trying to finish a book. She wanted it for just that reason. No one around except critters, and no internet to distract her," he said, sliding her a sideways glance.

"Is there indoor plumbing, or are we talking outhouse?"

Her expression was completely innocent. Too innocent. And he couldn't resist. "There is an outhouse, yes."

She blinked, and the innocent expression shifted to one of horror. The craziness of it all hit him again; a murderer was looking for her, and she was worried about the plumbing.

City girl.

And that should put a permanent damper on…whatever this was he was feeling. Because it was obvious that two people couldn't come from more opposite worlds, and the barrier between the two was huge. Maybe insurmountable. So unless she was the type for a casual fling with a short expiration date, which he very much doubted, he'd better get a grip.

"But it's only there for emergencies, like if the waterline freezes and ruptures. There's a real bathroom. I promise."

He wanted to laugh at her sigh of relief, but he didn't. He had no right to laugh at anything, not when he was the reason she was in this mess. But then, unexpectedly, she laughed. And it was a light, wonderful sound.

"I am a spoiled city girl, aren't I?" she said. "So is that why we're going there? You don't think your father will find us?"

He gave her another sideways look, trying to gauge how he should answer that. Looking back at the way ahead, picking up the pace a little, so they'd get there before it was full dark, he answered as best he could. "It's remote, but it's also in the ranch information, the brochures and online. He was never much on research, but he's been locked up awhile. Maybe he learned. So I can't say he won't find out about it. Whether he'd make the jump, I don't know. I don't know how his mind works. I never did." He stopped before he veered into self-indulgent whining he—and she—couldn't afford.

He also didn't mention the other reason, besides the remoteness, that he'd chosen the cabin. The fact that it was on a hilltop, with a clear view and an open field of fire on all sides, making it more easily defensible, was probably not something she wanted to hear.

Chapter 20

The ranch itself had felt strange enough to Ashlynn, but this place, this isolated spot without even another building in sight, was like nowhere she'd ever been before. Where she came from this wouldn't be a hill, it would be a mountain. But the mountains that towered above them not much farther on put the lie to that. People at work—including her brothers—teased her that she needed to get out of the city more, but she'd always blown it off. Why would she leave when she had everything she needed? Not like she was a skier, or a hiker, or a fledgling naturalist or anything.

Yet as she got out of the truck she found herself breathing deeply, as if this were some new kind of air, a kind she'd never taken in before. Found herself stretching, as if she'd been cramped up too long and the open space was something to relish. And oddly, since she was used to always being around people, she felt as if this unpopulated place was a release, a freeing from restraints she'd never really been aware of before.

She wondered if this feeling was what they'd been looking for, those people who'd struck out westward in the early days of the country. Then she almost laughed at herself, the tech-dependent geek, getting a glimpse of what had driven people to seek out the opposite, places where even the telegraph of the times didn't reach.

She reached back in for her case full of gear most of those long ago pioneers couldn't have even imagined possible, and her purse. Kyle had already pulled out the other bags, and was carrying them inside. She started to follow him up the two steps to the wide porch furnished with two Adirondack-style chairs and a table to the right of the door, and a comfortable looking porch swing to the left. And then she stopped, almost mid-step, as she realized what she wasn't seeing.

Power lines.

She backed up, looked around to confirm her suspicion.

Nothing but clear air. Nothing for even a bird to perch on except trees and brush. *You mean their natural perches?* She laughed at herself again, and wondered what it was about this place that had her doing that so often. It was a strange feeling, but not a bad one.

"Zoe? Did you see something? Hear something?"

It took her a moment to realize what—and why— he was asking. His father. Maybe following them. "Oh. No, no, nothing like that. I was just noticing…what isn't here. Like power lines."

She thought he might tease her about that being what she'd noticed, but he must have thought his jab about the outhouse had been enough. "There's a generator.

Propane tank's full, so it'll keep us going for a couple of weeks, twice that if we're careful about it."

Twice that? A...month? Was he really thinking they'd have to hide out here that long? Before she could ask he was going on, the idea of being isolated here for weeks clearly not bothering him in the slightest.

"Well," she said, trying to focus, "at least it's in a good clear spot."

He gave her a startled look. "I... I wasn't going to mention that. But it's the big advantage."

She nodded, still looking around, or rather, up. "I shouldn't have any trouble getting a signal."

"A signal?" Now he sounded bewildered, and when she glanced at him his brow was furrowed.

"You'll see, when I get set up."

He gave a sharp shake of his head before shrugging off whatever thought he'd had. "I put your things in the bedroom, if you want to go get settled in. I need to check out the area."

The bedroom. As in one? And only one? That thought distracted her, and it took a moment for the rest of what he'd said to register. "Check the area?" Her head snapped around and she looked down the hill they'd just come up. "You don't think he's here already, do you?"

"No," he said. "But I need to know what things look like now so I can tell later if anything's been disturbed."

"Oh."

That made perfect sense to her. It was also something she never would have thought of. She started to nod, then stopped when she saw what he was carrying. At some point he'd grabbed that rifle off the rack in the truck. She told herself she should be thankful he was being so cautious, but all she really was was nervous. And not just about the weapon.

She watched him go, registering how much she liked the way he moved, quick and easy, and the way he looked in jeans. But the biggest thing that hit her was that he was doing all this to protect her. Because his father had not threatened him, he'd threatened her. As a way to hurt him, yes, but still, it would have been easy for him to blow it off because it wasn't like she was anything more than a guest he'd been nice to, which his father had apparently misinterpreted.

Not that you wouldn't like to be more...

She shook her head sharply and ordered herself to focus. She had things to do.

She strode into the cabin, determined now. She scanned the interior, pleasantly surprised. The kitchenette in one corner was small, but obviously quite modern, with all the necessities, including a microwave and a mini under-the-counter refrigerator, plus the luxury of a coffee machine on one counter. In the main room, a large comfortable-looking leather couch was facing the big front windows, which gave her a view out over all that open space. It looked almost like a huge painting. Beside a small but fully stocked bookcase on the far side of the windows was a table big enough to be a desk, and she wondered if that was where the writer Kyle had mentioned had worked. It seemed a great location for it.

On the far wall was a huge stone fireplace, with firewood already on the grate, and more stacked in a cubby beside the hearth. A closer look told her it was open on the other side, too, into what she presumed was that bedroom Kyle had mentioned, given the door in the far corner.

That one bedroom.

She held on to her determination to focus on what had to be done. She crossed and opened that door, confirming her guess. The bedroom was more spacious than she'd expected, with a small sitting area in a bay window that looked out on the back side of the cabin toward a stand of trees some distance away.

Her suitcase sat on a large four-poster bed—she moved on quickly—and the fireplace did indeed open into this room, as well. Smart, enabling you to warm the entire place if you got a good fire going.

She was pondering where to set up her gear—she always did that first, since it was her priority, clothes and such could wait—when it hit her there might be a bigger priority. He'd brought in the other items from the truck, including the ice chest. Which implied food.

She walked back toward the kitchen. Opened the small fridge, which was not cold. Nor did the wall switch add anything to the fading light from outside. Which in turn made her realize there wasn't a screen in sight. She tried to tell herself that didn't bother her, but the slight twitchiness that came over her was hard to deny. Was she truly so addicted that the absence of the tech she was used to made her this edgy?

It's being out of touch when there's a killer looking for you.

She suppressed a shiver. True, her gear was all fully charged, and she had a backup battery pack just in case, but in total that would only get her a few hours, especially using the satellite connection.

Generator. He'd said there was a generator. Although

the FBI office at home had one in case of power failures, she'd never lived with one as the sole source of power. It had been a long time since she'd had to deal with the idea, and she had to think about it for a minute to remember the procedures there and try to apply them here. She guessed keeping usage to a minimum would be key. Which to her meant her electronics and probably the fridge had to be on. The lack of anything else she'd just have to get used to.

At that thought she went to the sink and turned the tap.

Nothing.

A sound from outside made her whirl around. The sudden splash of running water made her spin back. She instinctively moved to shut it off. Another sound, turned her toward the end of the kitchen. The refrigerator coming on. The place was coming to life. Belatedly, she realized the first noise must have been the generator coming on. Somehow she hadn't made the connection with the water coming on. She should have, clearly there were no city water pipes out here. So there must be a well or something. Which probably had a pump, which would need power.

Another, louder noise from behind made her jump and spin back yet again. Kyle stepped in through the front door.

She'd had about enough surprises.

And she hated that the first thing he had to do when he came inside was put that rifle on a rack next to the front door. As if it were as ordinary as hanging up a coat.

"Do people really live like this?" It came out harsher than she'd intended.

He drew back slightly. His mouth twisted upward at

one corner. "You city folks really do live in a bubble, don't you?"

It came out in a bit of an exaggerated drawl. She didn't blame him; she hadn't meant to snap like that. "I'm sorry. I'm just…edgy."

She looked away, hating that her eyes had started to sting with moisture, hating that she'd snapped, hating that she been jumping like a skittish cat at everything ever since she'd gotten here. Maybe he was right about that bubble, because she certainly wasn't handling this well at all.

At least she heard him coming—you couldn't sneak very well in cowboy boots on a wood floor—so she wouldn't jump again when he reached the kitchen. But then she did jump, because he came up close and unexpectedly hugged her. But she relaxed immediately. Because it felt wonderful.

"It's no wonder you're edgy," he said softly. "I'm so sorry I got you into this."

She didn't know if it was the hug or the note of guilt in his voice that did it, but she felt suddenly steadier. She leaned back to look up at him, careful not to pull away so hard that he let go. She didn't want him to let go.

"You didn't," she said. "Your father did."

"But he—"

"Is not your fault."

"Still, I should never have let you…get close enough for him to notice."

"Stop it. You didn't even know he was out. Besides," she admitted, "I think it was me who started it."

He went very still. After a moment he said quietly, "Did you?"

And suddenly she couldn't do it. She couldn't continue the charade. Not with him. He was the most innocent person involved in all this, and yet he was the one who had just uprooted his entire life to protect her. The very least she owed him was the truth.

"I know this is a cliché, but...we need to talk." She grimaced. "Or rather I need to, and you need to listen."

He let go of her then, and she immediately missed the warmth, the gentleness, the support. When she met his gaze he said, "Is this going to include your real name?"

She drew in a deep breath. "Yes. And some other things."

"All right."

She was amazed at how easily he accepted. Then, with a wry smile, she gestured toward the big couch.

"I think you'd better sit down."

Chapter 21

"Ashlynn Colton?"

Kyle repeated it slowly. He was staring at her, a little distracted by the utter earnestness in her eyes and expression. She looked as if she were relieved to finally be telling the truth.

"That's the only real lie I told you," she said, her tone matching her expression. "The rest was…by omission."

He leaned back on the couch, tilting his head slightly as he looked at her. "Into the finer points of deception, are you?"

He saw color rise in her cheeks, but she didn't look away. "I had no choice. I told you, there's a killer after me, too." She took a deep breath and added, "A serial killer."

Kyle went still. Very still. Finally, slowly, he asked, "Just what is that 'organization' you do research for?"

Another deep breath. This time she did lower her

gaze for a moment before she lifted it to his again, and answered. "The FBI."

He let out a harsh breath, and barely managed to stop an eye roll. Of course. Why not, the way his life had been going lately? But after a moment of sour acceptance it registered that she likely wasn't lying about the serial killer stuff. And with that his thoughts shifted abruptly. Once he'd gotten past the shock of these two things, another, more personal shock hit him.

She'd trusted him. Enough to tell him the truth. This quickly.

He looked back at her then. She was watching him warily. His mouth twisted wryly. "Aren't we a pair," he muttered.

She smiled, sort of. As if she were trying but couldn't quite make it happen. No wonder, if a killer like that was after her. Still, as he looked at her, he couldn't shake the feeling that there was more she hadn't said. Something in the way she was sitting, so straight and tense, her hands knotted together.

"Guess it's a good thing we came up here on a couple of fronts, then," he finally said when she didn't speak.

She finally spoke. "More than you know."

He studied her for a long, silent moment, becoming more certain with every second that she had another bomb to drop. A glance at her hands told him they were still clasped tightly together, so tightly her knuckles were white. So it was a bomb she was dreading dropping. Great.

"Dump it all, will you? What could be worse than having to watch out for two killers?" She still didn't speak. And that put an acidic edge in his voice. "Maybe you'd rather debate which is worse, having a serial killer looking for you, or having your own father wanting you dead?"

She winced slightly, but met his gaze. "Instead of saying something worse yet?"

What the hell could be worse? "Like?"

"Like having your father want you dead and then finding out one of the main suspects in the serial killer case is…your brother."

He gaped at her. He couldn't help it. "What?" he finally got out, and the single word rang with disbelief.

"It's true, Kyle, I'm sorry. Xander is a definite suspect in the Landmark Killer case."

The appellation—why the hell did they glorify those sickos by giving them catchy names?—rang a bell. He'd heard it before, in passing, somewhere, that the victims were all connected to famous landmarks in New York City. That kind of news wasn't something he followed so he'd not paid much attention, was just more grateful than ever that he didn't live in a place that spawned such people.

Except…maybe he did.

As the initial shock began to fade, his mind took off on several tangents at once, and all at high speed. He couldn't seem to latch on to any single one, and so the thoughts just ricocheted around in his skull. Inanely, the first one was shock that she knew he was related to the suspect. To Xander. Xander, a serial killer? He couldn't believe it. But why not? Not like he'd seen or even spoken to his half brother since Xander had left Montana over a decade ago. They'd barely spoken before that. In their entire lives Kyle doubted they'd spent more than a couple of hours together, and half of that in accidental meetings. The fact that they shared the same father did not make them close, as Xander had stated in so many words.

Kyle had always suspected that Xander resented the fact that their father had actually married Kyle's mother, but not his own. Not that it had made Kyle's life any better. In fact, worse in some ways.

Think you're better than me because the old man married your mother?

I think you're lucky he didn't marry yours. Trust me, you don't want the guy around.

That long-ago exchange with his half brother ran through his head. And he'd meant what he'd said. Victor Slater was not the kind of father you wanted to hang out with. He wasn't the kind you even wanted to acknowledge. And that had been before he'd become a killer.

But what if it wasn't? What if he'd killed someone else before and just not gotten caught?

That thought hadn't occurred to him, not until she'd mentioned a serial killer. Which sent him careening back to the idea that Xander might be one. Which brought on a final, horrifying thought…was it some kind of hereditary abnormality? Was there some kind of twisted or broken gene that got passed down, and turned people into killers?

Did he have it?

He felt a churning in his gut and a chill that had nothing to do with the October temperatures at the same time. He realized he was breathing faster and tried to slow it down. It was all he could do not to jump up and head outside for a long ride or hike, simply because that was what he did when he felt tense or restless. But he couldn't do that now. Not when his father might be out there.

His father the already known killer.

His father, who may have fathered another killer, an even worse one. A multiple murderer.

And who had fathered him.

Again he had to fight the urge to head out the door. He knew a little while out in the wild would calm him, it always did. But that wasn't—

"Here. Try this."

He was jolted out of his grim reverie by her quiet words. He stared at the mug she was holding out to him, full of a dark liquid. The last thing he needed right now was coffee, as wound up as he was, but…it didn't smell like coffee, even the fancy kind that came out of that type of coffee maker in the kitchen. He took a deeper sniff, and she apparently noticed.

"There were a couple of pods of hot chocolate out there. My guilty pleasure, when I'm too wound up for coffee."

He looked up at her as her words echoed his thought, realizing how totally out of it he'd been because he hadn't even been aware she'd gone to the kitchen and done this.

"I…thanks." He took the mug, and it felt good to even hold, the warmth chasing the chill out of his hands. The first sip did the same for the rest of him, and he felt, if not calm, at least better.

"I'm sorry, Kyle," she said. "Truly I am. But I couldn't think of a…kind way to say it."

He looked up at her, saw her expression was truly troubled. He gave a slow shake of his head and let out a sour chuckle. "You couldn't think of a kind way because there isn't one."

She resumed her seat on the couch, a couple of feet

away. Somehow this was more…intimate than the truck, even though she'd been closer there, distance wise. She held a mug of her own he finally noticed, although he thought he caught a whiff of a coffee aroma.

Because he couldn't think of anything else except getting into what he wasn't quite ready for yet, he thought of what she'd said when she'd given him the mug and said, "You're not too wound up for coffee?"

She smiled, although it still looked a little wobbly. "I have a lot to do yet tonight."

His brow furrowed. "To do?"

She drew in a deep breath, and sounded steadier when she went on. "I'm part of the team hunting the Landmark Killer. And as such, I…need to ask you some questions."

For a moment he just stared at her. And despite the ton of bricks she'd dropped on him here, all he could seem to think about was that now he knew why she'd been spending time with him. Not because she wanted to, but…because she had to.

The chill that enveloped him then was an entirely different kind than he'd felt before. And all he could think was that he was glad he'd found this out before he'd let his stupidity completely get the better of him, and had fallen for her. Although he should have known better in the first place. Sophisticated, big-city girl like her wasn't going to fall for an itinerate cowboy like him.

And that he'd thought that possible even for a moment was on him.

Chapter 22

"All right, Ms. Colton, FBI agent," Kyle said, leaning back on the couch. "Let's get this over with."

She supposed she couldn't blame him for the chill in his voice. Nothing like being told your brother was a serial killer suspect to put a damper on your mood, especially when you had already had to endure the pain of your own father murdering the woman you loved. She could have done without the formal "Ms. Colton," though. But she couldn't blame him for that, either. After all she had lied about her name. With reason, yes, but still…

She smothered a sigh, and wondered not for the first time how the field agents who went undercover managed to keep their emotions in check. Cash had once joked that they just had them surgically removed, and at the moment she was wishing that were really possible.

Because it's all about you, right? Kyle's been through

much worse, and he's not whining, is he? So you need to—what would they say around here?—buck up, maybe, and get this done and over with.

Self-lecture concluded, she tried to decide what to ask first. So many questions were spinning around in her mind she couldn't pin one down. This wasn't her bailiwick, interviewing people for information. Cash or Brennan should be doing this, or even Patrick, despite him telling her he was more comfortable with evidence that couldn't talk back.

And she proved her own inadequacy when the first thing she managed to say was, "I'm not an agent. I'm a researcher."

"Is that supposed to make me feel better? The alphabet letters are the same. And they don't impress quite like they used to."

She ignored that part, because she knew it was true and had no answer. "Look, I'm sorry I lied, but I had to."

"Let me guess. You were only following orders?"

She winced inwardly, but answered. "Yes. But they were orders from my family."

That made him draw back slightly. "Your family?"

She grimaced. "That alphabet agency is…sort of the family business. My three brothers, a cousin, and me."

His eyes widened. "Nepotism much?"

"I know it sounds like that, but it's not. They're all amazingly good at their jobs, two as field agents, one in forensics, and my cousin is a profiler. They're the best serial killer team in the country."

"And you do…what, the grunt work?"

That hit a nerve. "What I do is just as important. I give them the building blocks, the road signs, the clues. I follow the threads, find the leads."

He studied her for a moment, his expression unreadable. Then, in a tone she could only describe as loaded, he asked, "And what thread led you so far out of your comfort zone, Ms. Colton?"

She was such an idiot. She'd always envisioned interviews like this, with non-suspects, as calm, courteous affairs. They weren't suspects so they'd have no reason to be uncooperative, right? And most people would want to help, especially with a serial killer case. Some, she knew, even were excited to be involved, even tangentially.

Of course, in this case she'd expected it to be emotional, because it was a family member. But she hadn't expected it to be downright antagonistic.

Of course, she hadn't expected it to get all tangled up with her own emotions, either. And that was no one's fault but her own. She was the one who'd taken one look at him and had every cell in her body suddenly wake up, like a cliché on steroids.

She suddenly remembered the time another aide to FBI director Chang had come through and seen her and Xander at lunch, and teasingly asked if they were dating. She'd been startled at the very idea, because while he was cute, she wasn't attracted in that way to Xander at all.

His brother was a different story.

A different man. A very different man.

"So this questioning is going to be all one-way, is that it?"

His words startled her out of her mental rabbit hole. Another reason she'd be lousy at this; she couldn't seem to stop herself.

"No, I'm sorry, I was just thinking about...something else."

She had to focus to remember that he'd asked what thread had lead her here. And that made her realize she had yet another shock to deliver. And she had to decide whether to dole it out in bits, or just drop it all at once and get it over with. Something about the way he was watching her, warily yet determinedly, made her decide on the latter.

"I…know your brother, and what lead me here was something he said to me once."

He was gaping at her now, clearly shocked out of his understandable anger. "You know Xander?"

She nodded. "We work in the same building. In fact, he works for our boss, the director."

For a long, silent moment he just stared at her. And then, to her shock, he let out a short, sharp laugh. "You're telling me my half brother the serial killer suspect *works* for the director of the FBI?"

There was no doubt in her mind he hadn't known. There was too much disbelief in his tone, his expression. Still, she had to ask. "You didn't know he worked for the Bureau?"

"I haven't seen or talked to him since he left Montana over ten years ago. Longer, really, since we never talked anyway."

"Never?"

"Only if we ran into each other by accident, and then just long enough for him to be obnoxious."

Obnoxious? Xander? But he was charming. That was part of the reason she was having such a hard time believing he really was the brutal Landmark Killer. Was the charm all a front, to hide who and what he really was? It was hardly unusual for a killer to wear a convincing mask. Ted Bundy popped to mind.

Again she had to focus. Whatever knack her brothers had to zero in while conducting an interview she apparently lacked. Or maybe it was just because of who she was trying to interview, and the fact that he rattled her.

"Obnoxious…about what?"

"Me. My mother. Our home. Our life. He hated everything I love about Montana. The wide open spaces, the beauty of it, ranch life, the horses, all of it." His gaze narrowed slightly as he looked at her. "And he loved your stuff. The tech."

"Is that why you don't?" she asked, although it had nothing to do with the case, really. She was curious, she'd thought his apparent aversion was because it wasn't crucial in the life of a cowboy, either that or he was a cowboy because of that aversion.

"Probably," he admitted. "I mean, I've got a phone, but I'm happiest when there's no signal. Like here."

"That would drive me crazy," she admitted. *And aren't you going to be surprised when I get set up?*

"It drove Xander out of here. At least, that's what I always thought."

"So he went off to college?"

Kyle frowned. "No. He never went, couldn't afford it and didn't want to anyway. Last time I did see him, right before he got out of high school, he was mouthing off about how he didn't need it and it would bore him. I never saw him again."

Ashlynn frowned in turn; she was certain Xander had gone to an Ivy League school. Maybe he'd changed his mind after he'd left Montana. "So he just…left?" she asked.

Kyle nodded. "He couldn't wait to get out of here, he wanted the big city, where he thought he'd be a star."

His mouth twisted into a grimace. "Guess in a way he made it, huh?"

She supposed, in a way, he was right. She didn't say so but pressed on. "So you weren't...close?"

Another laugh, as harsh as the previous one. "Hardly. We had nothing in common except a sperm donor. You remember, the one that wants to kill you?"

She suppressed a shiver at that reminder. "Yes. I remember." She stood up abruptly. Since it seemed clear Kyle didn't know what his half brother had been up to since he'd last seen him, there was no point in badgering him. "I'd better get to work."

She walked over to where she'd set her gear case on the table by one of the big front windows. She opened it up and got out her laptop, then the satellite phone and the custom matched router that would make it the hottest of hot spots, no matter where she was. There were some excellent perks—for the tech oriented anyway—to working for the feds.

She realized Kyle had gotten up as well, and was now standing a couple of feet away, watching.

"That will really get you internet all the way out here?" he asked.

"Courtesy of your tax dollars," she said cheerfully.

"Nice to know," he retorted, with the usual sourness that topic brought out.

She was up and running in a manner of minutes. "Excellent," she murmured. "A good clear view of the sky."

Kyle made an odd sound. "That's what you meant when you said this was 'a clear spot' when we got here?"

"Yes," she said as she made the last connection. Then something about his tone registered and she looked at him, her brow furrowed. "What did you think I meant?"

"What I meant," he said flatly, "that this place is highly defensible, with a clear field of fire."

She felt a sudden chill as the reality of her situation bit deep. *Their* situation. A situation he'd put himself in to protect her.

Out of guilt, she reminded herself. He felt guilty, as if his father's actions were somehow his fault. As if it was his fault his father might be as unbalanced as his half brother. And therefore his fault she was in danger.

Belatedly it occurred to her that she could have resolved this simply by leaving. For anywhere. But at the same time she had a deep down feeling she was on to something. And realized this must be what her brothers felt like when they talked about having a hot lead. Like she had now.

And as she looked at the lean yet powerful man standing there, watching her with that steady gaze, she had the thought that there were hot leads, and then there was just plain hot.

And Kyle Slater definitely fell into the latter category.

Chapter 23

She was still at it.

Kyle had never understood the utter and total absorption with which some people could live through screens. Especially when there was such a beautiful living, breathing, real scene just outside the door. But absorbed she was, apparently not even noticing his pacing. Which was probably a good thing, because he didn't think he could stop.

Finally he decided the best thing he could do was make another circuit outside. He pulled on his jacket, reached into the backpack he'd left by the door to pull out the holster that held his bear spray and clipped it on his belt before taking the Winchester from the rack.

He pulled the door open. There was no moon, and the darkness was deep. He just stood there, listening for a moment. He heard nothing on this calm, clear night, and stepped out onto the porch. He scanned the open space before him, still listening. And still nothing unexpected. He checked the tree line in the distance, but saw nothing moving.

He stepped down from the porch, and for the first time looked up toward the sky. And stopped dead. He felt the usual tightening in his chest at the sight, as if in that moment nothing else mattered.

An impulse hit him, hard, and he was following it before he really thought. He turned back, opened the door and stepped back into the cabin. He started to speak, caught himself before he said "Zoe" and managed to get out "Ashlynn" instead. Not that it mattered, she was so intent on whatever was on her laptop screen—and she hadn't been kidding about that connection, whatever all that gear was, it worked—she merely murmured something unintelligible from here. So he crossed the room, stood behind her chair, and tried again.

"Ashlynn."

She jumped, clearly startled. "What?"

"Come with me. You need to see something."

Her eyes widened. "Is he here?"

"No, nothing like that."

She glanced back at her laptop as if she were reluctant to leave it. Since the only thing he could see on the screen was a stack of windows with rows of text and a browser with more tabs open than he'd ever seen in his admittedly limited experience, he wasn't sure what the lure was, but it made him think it was a good thing he'd followed this impulse. Because if she couldn't see the appeal of anything else, anything real, better he find out now.

Why that mattered, he didn't let himself think about. But she got up, and went with him to the door. He took her jacket from the rack and held it for her. She gave him a sideways glance but didn't say anything except thanks as she slipped it on. As she did he saw her gaze snag on the small canister on his belt.

"What is that, a water bottle or something?" she asked.

"Bear spray," he answered.

Her eyes widened and she took a step back. "Bear spray? There are...wild bears here?"

"Hate to break it to you, but there's no such thing as a completely tame bear. And yes, this is their turf." He didn't point out that that included the often cranky and aggressive grizzly, just went on. "And elk and mountain lions and moose and mule deer and bobcats and bighorn sheep and wolves and—"

He stopped when she held up a hand. "Okay, okay, I get it. Wildlife nirvana."

"Pretty much."

"Including snakes."

"Yes. But I'd worry more about wolverines, frankly."

Her eyes widened again. "Wolverine...like in the comic books and movies?"

His mouth twisted wryly. "In spirit and ferocity, maybe. Come on."

She hesitated. "I feel like I'm stepping into a zoo where all the enclosures have been left open."

"You're stepping into reality," he corrected. "It's the zoos that are unreal."

"Point taken," she admitted. Then she drew herself up and followed him outside. She might be a city girl to the bone, but she didn't lack for nerve.

"Besides," he said as they went down the porch steps, keeping her gaze on him, "it's not the wildlife I want you to look at."

"What, then?"

"You'll see."

If she was still hesitant it didn't show. So once she made her mind up, she didn't waver. She did, however, keep her eyes scanning the ground and the space before them, not above them. Which was okay with him because once he had her in the best spot he stopped. He touched her shoulder and pointed upward.

"This is why Montana's called Big Sky Country."

She looked up, and gasped. Even in the faint light he saw her head move as she tracked the incredible arc of stars and space dust that flowed across the lower sky in a narrow band, southwest to northeast.

"Oh! Is that...?" she asked, sounding astonished.

He managed not to laugh, but barely. "That, city girl who's probably never really seen the stars, is the Milky Way. You're looking at the galaxy we live in."

She continued to stare, as if stunned. "I've seen pictures, but..."

"Can't truly capture the real thing, can they?"

"No. No, apparently not."

"True about a lot of things. Reality beats the imitation."

"Don't lecture me now, please. I'm enjoying the real."

She said it as if she'd heard lectures like that all too often, so he shut up. She stood there looking at the arc of light and dust and gas for a long time. Then, quietly, she said, "This is almost better than those pictures, even the ones from the space telescopes."

"It gives you a better idea of how amazing it is, I think, to see it like this, as our ancestors did, with nothing but your eyes."

"Yes," she said, still sounding awed.

"We're lucky we have a clear night, and no moon. This isn't prime viewing season, in fact we're at the end of it."

He could almost hear the frown in her voice. "There's a season? I wonder why."

She hadn't said it as if she were asking him, but he answered anyway. "Because of the way the earth is angled at different times of the year, and that we're in one arm of the galaxy, not the center. So by next month, it'll be so close to the horizon you won't be able to see it because of earth's atmosphere."

She'd turned her head now. He could almost feel her staring at him. Finally she said, very quietly, "If that was to tell me I shouldn't assume you're some dumb cowboy, that wasn't necessary."

He started to retort, then stopped. Had it been? Had he reacted with that explanation to prove something? He'd encountered a lot of city folk since working here who made just that assumption, that living the life he so loved was somehow mentally limiting. Or only appealed to mentally limited people. Of course those city folk often included people who assumed anyone who didn't have a college or university degree but chose instead to actually work must be lacking on the intelligence scale. He was willing to bet she had one of those degrees on her wall, but she hadn't seemed like one of those people, even with her tech obsession.

"Don't forget," she went on, still quietly, "I've seen the books on your shelf."

"Library," he said, not sure what else to say. Then he shrugged. "Hard to lug along a big stack of books when you move around a lot."

"So you check them out a half dozen at a time? Everything from ancient philosophers to science fiction?"

"They're remodeling the library in Bozeman, so I get a lot at one time to stay out of their way." He wasn't sure why he was explaining all this.

"You need an e-reader. That way you can carry around thousands of books with you in less space than it takes to carry one paper book."

"It's not the same." *Nor is the cost.* His mouth twisted. "I'm surprised you didn't say just read on my phone."

"I would have, except I've seen your phone," she retorted.

He couldn't help it, he laughed. "I can see where my phone would seem pitiful to someone like you."

"Someone like me?" It was the same tone she'd had when she'd made the comment about lecturing her. And he wondered if she'd had a lot of those kinds of observations tossed at her.

"Someone who can come way out here and still connect to the internet, via some satellite passing by up there, between us and the rest of the galaxy."

She sounded completely different when she asked, "Is that a compliment, from you who doesn't care about the internet?"

Among all the other compliments I could pay you…

But he only shrugged—an instinctive but useless gesture out here in the dark—and said as casually as he could manage, "I can admire, and appreciate, even if I don't use it much. Sort of like even though I can't fly one, I can admire and appreciate a jet fighter."

Or admire and appreciate you, even if I don't dare say so.

Chapter 24

Although she found it hard to believe anyone could know her beloved internet and not be engrossed by it 24/7, Ashlynn admitted that sort of made sense. It was kind of like how she felt about the horses; she could appreciate their beauty and function, even though she was clueless about them on a day-to-day basis.

Besides, she also knew the downside of her world. There was more than enough bad stuff to go around, and it didn't take much searching to find it. Nobody knew that better than she did, given it was sort of her job to find it. So despite the online world she found so amazing, she was under few illusions about it's potential for evil.

Then again, it was hard not to be amazed by what she was looking at now. And she had to admit he was right, there was something about seeing it in person and not in an image rendered on a screen, that made it…more.

She didn't know how long they'd been standing there, only that cold was starting to creep in. She should have fastened up her coat before coming out here, it had to be in the thirties. She moved to do it now.

"Cold?" he asked, his voice oddly rough.

"A little bit," she admitted. "But this is so amazing I don't want to stop looking."

"I'm glad. I'd hate to have dragged you out here for nothing."

She glanced at him. Her eyes had adjusted to the darkness, and she thought she saw a slight smile curve his mouth. That mouth she'd been thinking about since the moment he'd popped up from behind Splash.

And then he moved, coming up close behind her and slipping his arms around her.

"Warmer this way," he said, and she told herself she was imagining the tone of his voice, a tone that implied he was feeling the same draw she was. But she felt the warmth he radiated immediately, and couldn't bring herself to pull away. Not that she wanted to, not at all, but she should, shouldn't she? She was here on a case, not to…

Not to what? Fall for a cowboy she'd known for all of two days? Fall for a cowboy at all? If there were ever two lifestyles that were unmeldable, theirs had to be the two. But she understood now, as she never had before, the appeal of being out of the city, of being in the middle of…all this.

Or maybe it was simply his appeal, which at the moment, as he stood with his arms around her, overcoming the chill with his closeness, seemed as powerful as the view before her. And she felt a sudden rush of gratitude that he had, as he'd put it, dragged her out here for this.

"Thank you," she said. "For dragging me out here."

His arms tightened around her slightly in response. When he answered, his low, slightly rough voice was so close to her ear it almost made her shiver all over again. "You're welcome."

And before she even realized she was doing it, she was leaning back against him, savoring his heat, and the solid strength of that lean, muscled body. And for the first time since this case had begun, she didn't feel the consuming urgency to get back to her laptop and continue her searching. For now, all she wanted to do was to stay right here, with that glorious sight before her and strong, welcome arms around her.

Finally, he was the one who moved. "It's going to be down to freezing shortly, if it's not already," he said. "We'd better get back inside."

With a reluctant sigh she agreed. But the moment they stepped back into the cabin and the warmth from the fire he'd built earlier enveloped her, she couldn't help smiling.

"What?" he asked.

She looked at him. Nodded back toward the door they'd come through. "That was huge and magnificent, and I'm really glad you showed me. But I like warm and cozy, too."

Here in the light she could see that his jaw tightened momentarily before he said levelly, "Lot to be said for warm and cozy."

Oh yes, there was.

Once shed of their outerwear, she walked over toward the fireplace to warm up some more. And to try and rein in—there she went with horse metaphors again— her careening response to his words, his voice…him.

Kyle went into the small kitchen and she heard him moving things. She stood in place, savoring the heat even as she thought she'd enjoyed the heat he generated more.

Trying to distract herself, she wondered if she could build a fire. She should have watched him do it at least.

You did watch. You just weren't paying attention to what he was doing, but how he moved while doing it.

With that thought she was almost warm enough to step away from the fire when he came back into the room, holding two mugs. He handed her one, with a smile that seemed charmingly shy.

"We're going to run through the hot chocolate supply fast, at this rate."

She was taking her first sip of the luscious brew when something suddenly struck her. Her eyes wide, she looked up at him. "How much do they charge to rent this place?"

He looked a little startled. "Uh…less than your place, since it's so far out and a little thin on mod-cons. Why?"

"I'm sorry, I didn't even think about you having to pay for this place, and—"

She stopped when he held up a hand. "I'm not. I told you I have a great boss. It's almost never rented anyway this time of year, so he told me to use it as long as necessary."

She stared at him. Tried to imagine any landlord in the city doing something like that. Couldn't. But all she could manage to say was, "So he…knows?"

Kyle nodded. "Had to tell him, since my father was hanging around the ranch. I was afraid somebody might get hurt if they didn't know not to treat him like some casual trespasser."

"And how do you treat a…casual trespasser here?"

Kyle shrugged. "Shoot 'em." Her eyes widened even further. Kyle rolled his. "Isn't that what you expected to hear?"

She sighed. "Could we stop the city versus country dialog, for a while, at least?"

"Sorry."

"How would you feel if you had to go to my home ground?"

"New York City? Trapped, I guess. Hemmed in by all those towering buildings. Depressed at never being able to see more than a patch of sky at a time."

"And not expecting to find anything you liked about it?"

"Pretty much," he admitted.

"That's how I felt, coming here. But then…you showed me differently." She nodded back toward the door. "With that." She smiled then. "Well, that and the horses."

He started to speak, then stopped, as if he wasn't sure what to say. Finally he just gave a one-shouldered shrug and said, almost awkwardly, "I miss that darn Splash."

"And sweet Daisy?"

"Her, too."

"I'm not surprised. You're so good with them. When I first arrived, they told me you were the one to see if I had horse questions."

He blinked. "They did?"

She nodded. "Said you knew more than the rest of them put together."

"Who said that?" he asked, a touch of disbelief in his voice.

"Older man, with a serious moustache."

"Silver hair?" She nodded again, and he smiled. "Oh. Elliott. Yeah, he might have said that."

"Friend of yours, then?"

"I hope so. I…really admire him." He shrugged again, lowering his eyes. "I admire everybody at the ranch. They've been really decent to me, more than I deserve."

She found the element of doubt in the words achingly sad. But having grown up with the kind of father he'd had, perhaps not surprising.

"You're wrong," she said gently. His gaze shot back to her face. "You deserve that, and more. No matter what your father told you."

He grimaced. "He's more a pound it into you kind of guy."

She wasn't surprised that Victor Slater had been physically abusive to his son, as well. That Kyle had turned out as he had, protective—even of someone he'd only just met—kind, and gentle enough to get a young horse no one else could handle to respond to him, was amazing. Beyond amazing.

But that made her think of Victor's other son. She was surprised at how well Xander had hidden the apparent misery of his childhood. Which only emphasized that he might be quite capable of hiding much more. Just how far had his deceit gone?

She needed to get back to work and find out.

Chapter 25

"Tell me you're not still working."

Kyle stifled a yawn as he got up and stretched. He'd caught maybe six hours on the couch, enough to keep going. Just. But Ashlynn was in the same spot she'd been in when he'd finally drifted off, sitting at the table with all that gear of hers, her right hand on the computer mouse and her eyes fixed on that damned screen.

"Again," she said after a moment, sounding rather vague.

He walked toward her as he said, "What?"

"Working again, not still. I slept for a little while."

Only then did he realize she was wearing a different sweater, this one a warm gold color. And her hair was piled on top of her head, held crazily in place by…a pencil?

He blinked as he got closer, staring. How on earth

did a pencil stabbed through that big mass of hair hold it all in place?

And what would it look like if I pulled that pencil out and let it all cascade down—

He stopped his brain from charging down that path with an effort. More of an effort than he could remember ever having to make when his mind wandered down corridors it shouldn't.

"Define 'a little while' for me."

She gave him a sideways look. He thought it looked a little sheepish, knew it looked weary; those lovely brown eyes were tired. "A couple of hours," she said. Then, openly sheepish this time, she added ruefully, "Face down on the keyboard, I'm afraid."

"I'm not surprised." He hesitated, then risked it. "Doesn't being exhausted lead to...well, mistakes?"

She let out a disgusted sigh, and he guessed he'd made her mad. Maybe she never made mistakes when it came to this work. But then she let go of the mouse, leaned back in the chair, and rubbed at her temples.

"Yes," she said. "Yes, it does. But sometimes, when I can just see a clue, the beginning of a trail, it's hard to stop."

He resisted yet another urge and this time thought for a moment before he said, "It's kind of like that with Splash. When he does something we've been working on for weeks right for the first time, it's really tempting to keep going, keep pushing, like pounding the lesson home."

She turned in the chair then and looked up at him. "But you don't?"

"I've found with him it sticks better if we stop right

there, I gush over him a bit, and then he gets to play. Then next time we start from there and move on."

She tilted her head slightly, and in a tone he found a little too intent for the subject, she asked, "Do you do that with every horse you work with?"

"No. Each horse is different. That's just what works best with him."

She gave him a smile that set off those thoughts again. "And that," she said, in a voice that revved up those thoughts even more, "is why you're so good at what you do. You know each case is different, because there are individuals involved."

He shrugged, but looked pleased. "Well, yeah. They're animals, but they're still individuals."

Her mouth twisted wryly, but it was still lovely. "That was one of the hardest things for me to learn. That even the perfectly written program or code could go sour because nothing's perfect for everyone, or every purpose."

"And not everyone, including me, speaks your language?"

"Exactly. Just as I don't speak…horse."

He laughed. And she had the crazy thought that she could be perfectly happy with anything, as long as she could hear that laugh. And if she could be the one to cause it, well…

She heard an odd little sound, a sort of gurgling growl, and embarrassedly realized it had come from her stomach. She needed to eat, something at least, but she needed to work, too. She was certain she'd hit something that didn't track, and she wanted to start digging.

"Heard that," he said with crooked smile. Then, unexpectedly, he added, "I'm not much of a cook, but I'm pretty decent with scrambled eggs."

She remembered the carton of eggs that she'd taken out of the cooler and put into the fridge once it was cold. He'd walked in on her putting things away, given her a raised brow and had said, "How domestic of you."

"Don't get used to it," she'd fired back.

It hadn't been until later that she'd played it back in her head and realized how "domestic" that teasing exchange had actually sounded.

She'd never been like that. With anyone.

She came out of her reverie realizing he was looking at her, waiting for an answer. Awkwardly she said, "You'd cook…for me?"

"I'm hungry, too. No big deal to fix a little more." Again with the shrug. She was starting to notice that it came more often when he said or did something nice. Which, all things considered, happened more often than she ever would have expected. After all, she'd both lied and been the bearer of bad news since the beginning.

Which, she reminded herself yet again, had been all of not quite three days ago now. She went back to work as he headed for the kitchen. Or at least, she tried to; just having him under the same roof was…distracting.

When he brought her a plate of eggs and sausage and set it down on the table she was using, she thanked him, thinking she could eat and continue to work. But her first bite of the eggs grabbed her full attention. She took another, going slower this time. Then she looked at him.

"These are wonderful. I've never tasted such flavor in scrambled eggs."

He shrugged yet again. "Touch of honey mustard. Something Sarah used to do."

She felt her throat tighten a little. What he'd been through in his life… She dealt with ugliness all the time in her work, but she was a safer two steps back. She certainly was not hit by it as the victims and their families were, but neither did she have to deal with the aftermath firsthand as her brothers did. No, she was safely behind her screens, acknowledging the ugly that happened but not having it haunt her.

Kyle had lived it. Was living it. First his father's abuse, then the murder of his girlfriend. Yet he never stopped caring for the animals in his charge, took the time and effort to help the little boy she'd read about break through the cloud of grief, handled sweet Daisy and fractious Splash with the same patience and gentleness.

And now he'd upended his entire life to protect her from that father. Her, the woman who'd told him his half brother might be a serial killer. The woman he was here cooking for.

Involuntarily her gaze flicked to the rifle beside the door. He hadn't just upended his life to protect her, he was risking it.

She was seized with a renewed sense of urgency. She needed to get back on the trail. She needed to prove or disprove that Xander was their man, or at the least come up with a lead for the team to follow. The sooner she could do that, the sooner Kyle could get back to his life, without this awful cloud hanging over him.

She realized that part of her urgency to do this was because she couldn't do anything about his father, at the moment. She didn't even want to think about it, because of the horror of what could be the final scenario in that case, of Kyle having to use that rifle on his own father to save her.

And it gave her an odd little shiver of feeling she couldn't quite describe to acknowledge that if it came to that, he would do it. She understood that the goal here was to stay safe until the authorities could round Victor up, but if he found them, if it came down to it… she had no doubt what Kyle would do. Even after only three days, she was certain.

Maybe she had some of the instincts about people her brothers wielded so well after all.

Or maybe she was completely wrong. It wouldn't be the first time she'd misjudged someone. People were, as Kyle had said about the horses, individuals, and sometimes she didn't quite understand why they reacted the way they did, to many things. They were unpredictable, and she found that frustrating. It was why she preferred her tech; if something went wrong, it was usually just a matter of digging and backtracking, or a simple update to fix it.

If she was wrong about Kyle, she could end up dead.

But she wasn't. She just knew she wasn't.

And if she kept seeing in her mind the countless reports of people, family members, neighbors, witnesses, who had said the same thing over the years she'd been doing this, it somehow still didn't rattle her certainty.

If she was wrong about Kyle she had no business doing this work.

Or at least, no business doing it in person, where apparently a pair of deep brown eyes, kindness and a gentle knack with other creatures was all it took to convince her he was nothing like his father. Or his half brother.

Sometimes you just go with your gut, because it's all you've got.

Brennan had told her that once, when trying to explain why he'd been so certain of their suspect in a previous case, when in fact there hadn't been much evidence. Her mind, trained to follow concrete data, had trouble wrapping around that idea.

But now, with nothing more than that same kind of gut-level certainty, she was risking her life that she was right.

Chapter 26

Kyle looked up yet again from the book he'd been trying to read. He usually had no trouble with this popular
thriller series, but he was apparently too distracted to
focus at the moment. Either that or the author had left
out a crucial bit of explanation that made what the hero
of the book had just done understandable, and since that
had never happened before he figured it must be him.

Maybe he should have packed that volume on Aristotle.

His gaze shifted to Ashlynn—the name Zoe still
popped into his head when he looked at her—who was
still glued to her screen. She seemed to alternate between periods of simply staring and moments of mad en-
ergy, typing fast and using the mouse for multiple clicks
in a row. He could almost sense she was on the trail of
something, and how each step led her to another step.

Occasionally she would even resort to writing something down on paper, which surprised him, but when
he asked she said it was for things she wanted to go
back to but didn't dare stop her train of thought to do at
that moment. That made sense to him; more than once
when he'd been out tracking a wandering cow he'd noticed something else that needed attention, like a leaning fence post or a patch of poison hemlock that needed
to be cleared out, but finding the lost cow was the first
priority so he'd made mental notes.

*She's going so fast and deep that mental notes prob-
ably get crowded out.*

That she was hunting Xander still boggled him. His
half brother had always been a volatile sort, but Kyle
had always put it down to him hating both his father and
Montana. And while he couldn't understand the latter,
he certainly could the former, since he wasn't fond of
the old man himself, even before he'd shattered Kyle's
life by murdering Sarah.

But Xander, a serial killer? He just couldn't wrap his
mind around it. Now, as he watched her work, it tickled the edges of his mind again, that idea that with a
murderous father who had a possibly murderous son,
wasn't it possible—maybe even likely—that Victor had
passed on some sort of twisted genetic predisposition
toward the act? A predisposition he himself might have
inherited as well?

He tossed down the book and stood up. He needed to
make another security check. Because he had to move,
to do something, not because he thought they'd been
found. There'd been no sign of anyone around. The
closest human being he'd seen had been someone riding leisurely along the stream far below, and his father

had never sat a horse in his miserable existence. Probably one of the things that had pushed Kyle toward this way of life, although his love of horses would have been enough.

Ashlynn didn't even look up as he left the cabin. Once outside where he could breathe in that crisp, fall air, he immediately started to feel calmer. He made the circuit he'd established, and saw nothing different except some fresh droppings he guessed were deer or elk. Which told him in turn there likely wasn't a predator for those species close by at the moment. One less thing to worry about, although that could change at any time.

But the predator he was worried about had two legs, not four.

Ashlynn sat staring, unable to quite believe what she'd discovered. She leaped to her feet, wrapping her arms around herself as she started to pace. It wasn't possible. It just wasn't.

And yet there it was. Three different trails, and they all led to the same unavoidable conclusion. The same unavoidable yet impossible conclusion.

She suddenly realized she was alone in the cabin. On that thought she vaguely remembered hearing Kyle leave a while ago, on one of his frequent perimeter checks, as he called them. It had made her smile because it sounded like something her brothers would say, but the smile faded because of the reason for those perimeter checks.

You should have at least pulled out of it enough to tell him to be careful. Not that he isn't, but at least you could show him you appreciate what he's doing, and that he's doing it for your sake.

The moment the self-chastisement finished romping through her head, another thought followed on its heels. One that hadn't occurred to her before, but should have. So when, to her relief, Kyle stepped through the doorway back into the cabin, she hit him with it without really thinking about it.

"What would your father do if I hadn't been around?"

He stopped in the act of pulling off the knit hat he'd put on for warmth, quite necessary she judged from the rush of cold air that followed him in.

"What?"

"If your father had come looking for you and I hadn't been here, at the ranch I mean, what would he do? If he hadn't…thought what he'd thought, about us."

She saw his jaw tighten as he finished pulling off the hat, then his heavy jacket, and hung them both on the rack by the door. And through some combination of reading his expression and a few years of studying the psyches of killers, she guessed the answer.

"He said he's going to kill you, didn't he? For testifying against him."

"Pretty much a given." It came out flatly, in a sort of growl. "He promised that right after the trial."

"But now…"

"He only threatened you because he wants to be sure I suffer as much as possible beforehand."

"Didn't you tell him it wasn't true? That…it's not like that, between us?"

For an instant something flashed in his eyes, something that made her wonder if he, too, had been feeling that same kick of attraction she'd been feeling since the moment she'd seen him popping up behind Splash. But it was gone too quickly for her to be sure. And his next words crushed the idea.

"I told him you were just a guest at the ranch. That I had to be nice."

Of course. When in doubt, go with the truth. "And?" she asked, a tiny bit proud that she'd managed such an unemotional tone.

He held her gaze then, and once more she saw that glint that hinted at...something. "He didn't buy it," he said coolly.

Her first thought was that maybe Victor had been looking at her, not his son. Not because she was anything special to draw his eye, but...maybe he'd seen in her expression what she was feeling. For his son. And decided he had another target that would allow him to watch his son suffer.

Again.

And suddenly her thoughts now collided with what she had just learned, and she felt more than a little queasy. She reached out blindly for the chair she'd been sitting in, not realizing she'd stepped too far away from it in her pacing.

Kyle was there in what seemed like an instant, preventing her from falling ignominiously on her backside.

"Ashlynn?"

The feel of his hands steadying her and the concern in his voice made her eyes sting. Because no matter what else might be only in her imagination, that concern was real. He might have only brought her here, might have only felt he had to protect her because it was his father who was after her, but this simple concern was real.

"I'm...sorry," she said after a moment. "A couple of things hit my brain at the same time."

"Must have hit pretty hard," he said, his tone lighter now as he pulled over the chair for her. She sat, gratefully.

"They did." She sucked in an audibly deep breath.

He was crouched in front of her now. "Going to tell me?"

He sounded as if he half expected her to say no, but that seemed so wrong when he was so…entwined in all this. So wrong that she wouldn't—couldn't—say it, even though she was sure her brothers would tell her she should.

"It was the juxtaposition of what your father is and… what Xander likely is."

His expression changed. As if some horrible, unbearable thought had hit him. And considering what he'd been through recently, it had to be pretty bad to make him look like that. She was about to ask when his gaze flicked to where her laptop was still showing the last screen she'd been on. And when he looked back at her, she saw understanding in his eyes.

"You found something." It was statement, not question, but she answered anyway.

"Yes."

"What?"

"I found that Xander faked everything. Every application document, every written recommendation, every reference he provided was fabricated. The phone calls made to references were all routed differently, but ended up in the same place. The signatures on letters were forged. His entire background and résumé, everything that got him hired at the Bureau, was faked."

He stared at her. "Fake…but good enough to get past the FBI?"

"That's how good he is. And he'd have to be very, very good—and smart—to get past our screeners."

He stared at her. Then said, in the grimmest tone she'd ever heard, "And to get away with multiple murders."

"This isn't really proof of that," she cautioned. "People do occasionally fake their way in." She grimaced. "Although I can't think of a better way to throw off suspicion."

He straightened up then, and rubbed at his face, his eyes, as if he were exhausted. He probably was.

"This," he said sourly, "is why I deal with horses. Humans are seriously messed up."

She couldn't think of a thing to say. Because she knew the truth of his words better than most.

Chapter 27

The situation was so insane he almost wanted to laugh. Here he was, holed up in a remote cabin hiding from his father, who was a convicted killer, suddenly face-to-face with the genuine possibility his half brother was even worse, a serial killer. Then again, maybe Xander wasn't worse. After all, it had been his father who had made the threat that had driven them here, a threat that indicated he was more than willing—and Kyle had no doubts that he was able—to become a serial murderer himself.

And once more he had to quash down the fear that there truly was some genetic fault that Victor Slater had passed on to Xander. Which could mean there was an even chance he'd passed it on to him, too, despite Ashlynn's faith. A faith he wasn't sure he deserved.

He glanced at Ashlynn, who was typing rapidly into what looked like some sort of email or messaging program. Not that he would know.

She hit one last key with a bit more emphasis, and he thought he heard her mutter, "There."

Then she leaned back in the chair and rubbed at her temples again.

"Your eyes could probably use a break," he suggested.

"Oh, they could," she said, swiveling in the chair to look over to where he sat on the couch, his feet up on the coffee table as he tried to slog his way through the mental morass he found himself in. "Especially since I didn't put on my computer glasses."

His head tilted slightly as he tried to picture her in glasses. Something trendy and citified, no doubt. "Computer glasses?"

"I don't need regular eyeglasses—yet, anyway. But these are especially designed just for computer work, to ease the eyestrain so that it stays that way. But I… forgot."

He studied her for a moment, then gave her a lopsided smile. "Should I translate that as you got so far down a rabbit hole so fast it didn't even occur to you?"

"Exactly," she admitted, smiling back.

That they were able to smile under the current circumstances was amazing. Or special. Or…well, it meant something. Didn't it?

As if that thought had breached a barrier, the question burst through. "Is there some kind of serial killer gene?"

Her eyes widened. She knew with sudden certainty that he was very afraid of the possibility that there was, and that his father had passed it on. To him. And she could see why; if it could go from father to one son, then why not the other?

Without speaking she got up and came over to sit beside him. Close enough that it rattled him a little. Then she reached out and took his hand in hers. And that rattled him even more. It felt so good. So right. Really right. He told himself yet again he was being a fool when she went on earnestly, clearly trying to comfort him.

"You'd have to talk to my cousin, Sinead, who's a profiler, if you want a scholarly answer to that," she said. "But if the real question is do *you* have the gene if there is one, or even a tendency, then I can answer that one, unequivocally. No. You do not."

He stared at her. "How can you be so sure?"

"Because I am. I'm utterly certain. And if I'm wrong, then I deserve what I get."

"That's a bit…arbitrary."

Her grasp on his hand tightened, and he couldn't stop himself from looking down, just to see her fingers curled around his.

"I might not be an expert in profiling, but I've read enough of the results, been through enough cases to see the markers. The clues along the way, that people miss because they're not looking for them."

"You said yourself you didn't see them in Xander."

She made a tiny, disgusted sound, clearly aimed at herself. "I'll dispense with the 'we're still not sure' routine and admit I wasn't looking," she said, sounding beyond rueful. "Because I trusted the screening process, more fool me."

"What are you trusting now?"

"Myself. And you. How you are with people, with the horses. You are not one of them, Kyle Slater."

He looked back up at her then. Not knowing how to explain how much her certainty eased his turmoil, he just said, "I hope you're right."

She leaned back against the couch. "I am." She smiled. "You don't even have that famous redhead temper."

He went still. "The hell I don't," he muttered, his just acquired ease vanishing abruptly. "I've got it. And I've spent my life trying to keep a lid on it, because I didn't want to be like…him."

"And you've succeeded," Ashlynn said. "Don't you see, Kyle? That's the difference. People like your father, and maybe Xander, can't do that. They don't have the capacity to control themselves."

"Xander sounds pretty controlled, if he is your Landmark Killer and has gotten away with it for this long."

She looked thoughtful for a moment. He appreciated that about her, that she didn't dismiss what he said out of hand because he wasn't part of her world. "That's an excellent point. Was he controlled when you knew him?"

He let out a harsh laugh. "Hardly. I think he hated me most of all, and he never hesitated to let me know it."

Her brow furrowed. "He hated you more than your father?" He nodded. "Why?"

"Because the old man at least married my mother." He grimaced. "For all it gained her, which was nothing but pain. But Xander resented that. He told me once that he knew I thought I was better than him, because they were married."

"What did you say?"

"I asked him if he really thought I liked being tied legally to that…well, never mind what I called him."

A slight smile flickered over her face, but her tone was still very serious when she asked, "Did he ever get over thinking that?"

"I doubt it. I think it got worse after his mom did get married when he was still a kid, and he hated that guy,

too. Even more than our father, I think. Or at least…
more viciously. Wished him gone more than once."

"Seems the problem might be with him," she said, her
mouth quirking.

He rubbed his free hand—no way was he pulling
his other hand from hers—over his tired eyes. "I don't
think I've ever seen him…happy."

"You see?" she said gently. "That's another reason
I know you're not one of them. I've seen how happy
you are, here, with the horses. And the compassion you
had for that little boy who was here, who'd just lost his
brother."

He blinked. "You know about that, too?"

"I saw it in a review of this ranch. A glowing review,
I might add. Of the ranch, and you."

"Oh."

He didn't know what else to say. It gave him an odd
feeling to think his name was out there, floating around
the internet, when looking up a word he didn't know
when he came across it in his reading was about as far
as he went.

For a moment she just sat there, brow slightly furrowed, in the manner that he'd come to understand
meant that agile brain of hers was racing. More importantly to him at this moment, she didn't let go of
his hand.

After a long, silent pause, sounding hesitant, she
asked, "Did your mother ever…interact with Xander?"

His own brow furrowed, wondering why that mattered. "She knew he existed. And she saw him once or
twice that I know of, but I don't think it was ever anything but at a distance."

"And you and Xander didn't interact as brothers?

When you were kids, I mean, you didn't play together or anything?"

He nearly snorted. But he still didn't move his hand. "No. He wanted nothing to do with me, and vice versa. If I saw him in time, I usually dodged him instead. Especially if he was with his family, because they ticked him off and I knew he'd be spoiling for a fight."

He wasn't at all sure why he was talking about this to her, he never did. To anyone. For the most part, he didn't even think about those days that seemed eons ago. But something about this woman seemed to have him vomiting out all the grim details of his childhood. Or maybe it was just the way she kept holding on to his hand, something about the connection between them.

And maybe you're just a fool, Slater.

"What about your mom? Do you still have contact with her?"

He hadn't expected that one. "A little." His mouth twisted. "She tries, anyway. I'm not the best at keeping in touch with her. She moved to Ohio after my father went to prison, to live with her sister." He shrugged. "Can't blame her for wanting to get away from here."

"But you stayed."

"Call me stubborn."

She looked at him for a long moment, and her mouth—that darned mouth he couldn't stop thinking about—curved into a slight smile. "I have a list of things I'd call you. And I'd go for tough rather than stubborn."

He wanted very much to ask what else was on that list.

But he didn't. Because it might lead down a path he had no right to take.

Chapter 28

Ashlynn became aware of three things in succession as she slowly woke up. She was delightfully warm, felt oddly safe, and...she was snuggled up to—almost on—Kyle.

That jolted her fully awake. They'd ended up stretched out on the couch together, although she wasn't quite sure how. She could feel his chest move in the deep, regular breathing of sleep, as one arm was wrapped around her, holding her securely. And since there was faint light coming through the windows, they had apparently spent the rest of the night that way.

She was glad she hadn't awakened him with her little start, because she needed a moment to calm herself down from the unexpected—but not unwelcome?—realization of their rather intimate position.

She didn't know how to feel. Or more accurately, she

didn't know how to feel about how she was feeling. Because nothing had ever felt so right.

Well, that was a tangled mess. Maybe you're still asleep and just dreaming this. But why would you dream about it unless...you wanted it?

Normally she would have gotten up and run cold water over her face to wake herself up so she could think rationally. But she didn't want to get up. Wasn't even sure she wanted to think rationally, if it meant giving up this wonderful sensation of warmth and safety and comfort.

That she felt it now, when being hunted by a man who had already killed once, seemed absurd, but she couldn't deny it.

The moment she thought about Victor Slater a memory struck her, of the last thing she could remember thinking before—apparently—she'd fallen asleep practically on top of Kyle.

Now she did sit up. Carefully, trying not to wake him up. She needed to think, and clearly, and she couldn't seem to do that when she was so close to him. He stirred slightly, but didn't wake. She got to her feet and backed away, watching him. When she was far enough away she turned, tiptoed into the bathroom and closed the door. She turned on the cold water and reached down to cup some in her hands. And had to smother a small shriek. Apparently cold well water in Montana in October was rather different than cold city water in New York. She was surprised it was running at all, because ice couldn't be much colder.

She was tempted to use some hot water, but chided herself out of it.

"Chicken," she muttered to herself, and went for the

icy splash over her face. She shuddered under the impact, and grabbed hastily for a towel from the rack beside the sink.

"Ashlynn?" Kyle's voice came through the closed door. "Are you okay?"

Had she woken him after all? Or had he realized, even asleep, that she was gone and…missed her?

"I heard you yelp."

Well that should teach you. You didn't smother that shriek as well as you thought.

"I'm…fine. The water's just really cold."

"Well…yeah. It's snowing."

She blinked. Turned around and pulled the door open. He was standing just outside. "It is?" She hadn't even looked outside. It was never her first thought upon waking, maybe because the view out of her fifth-floor walkup never changed.

He nodded. "Started an hour or so ago, judging by what's on the ground."

"That's a good thing, isn't it? For us, I mean?"

He shrugged. She was getting tired of the gesture. But before she could ask him—rather snippily she was sure—what that was supposed to mean, he did actually answer. "Might slow him down a bit. But he was born and raised in Montana, so this little touch won't bother him much."

"Thank you."

He drew back slightly. "For what?"

"For not expecting me to interpret a shrug."

To her surprise he looked embarrassed. "Sorry," he muttered, lowering his gaze to his feet. "I do that when I'm thinking about what to say."

That quickly her entire outlook on it changed. She'd

always interpreted it as avoiding an answer, or an expression of doubt. She'd never thought of it as simply an indication a mind was working. And she certainly knew he had a mind that worked, and worked well.

"I wish more people thought before they talked." He looked up quickly, seeming even more embarrassed, so she tried for a teasing tone. "Just like I wish more people read Aristotle."

That got her a smile. "I got hooked on him when I learned he envisioned a far southern continent long before we knew it really existed."

She blinked. "He did?"

"In about 350 BC," he said. "And called it an Antarctic region."

"Hence Antarctica," she said, fascinated.

He nodded. "And that's why there's a range named the Aristotle Mountains there."

Her mouth quirked. "Given my reaction to the water here, I'm guessing I would not do well there."

A brief grin flashed across his face, something she would give a great deal to see more of. "Neither would I. Montana's cold enough, thanks."

She smiled back at him as she used the towel to finish drying her face and hands.

"Ever wonder why the expressions 'cold as hell' and 'hot as hell' both work?"

He said it in the tone of one musing idly about some mental puzzle that had just occurred to them. In the tone she often used herself, because she so often found herself doing the same. And somehow this thing they apparently had in common struck a chord deep inside her heart and mind.

"That's exactly the kind of rabbit hole I've been known to plunge into," she admitted.

"I kinda thought you'd get it," he said, and the smile he gave her then was somehow even more impactful than that lovely, flashing grin. Maybe because it was more pointed, more…personal. He might grin at anyone's attempt at a joke, but that smile…that smile was for *her*.

For a long moment he just stood there, looking at her. Then, abruptly, he broke the eye contact. "I'm going to make another circuit outside."

She fought down a jab of disappointment, not even certain what it was about. "Now? In the snow?"

"Snow makes it easier to spot footprints," he said, which she supposed was true.

And when he'd gone, it occurred to her to wonder if he even knew how they'd spent the night, wrapped together like…lovers. After all, he'd been asleep when she'd gotten up, maybe he had no idea she'd been there. So close. So very close.

She didn't know if that idea made her feel better or worse.

She spent an unknown amount of lost time trying to talk herself out of her own reaction to this man. It just wasn't like her to get like this so quickly. She needed time, she had to think, to analyze, she just did not fall for a guy in a matter of days. She hadn't even been here a week, and she was thinking about him…like this? It was so unlike her it made no sense. This uncertainty had her so on edge, when she was already stressed about the Landmark case, that she was doubting her own thought process.

You were wrong about Cash and Valentina. You never imagined they'd get back together.

The sudden thought about her brother and his exwife rattled her even further. What did she even know about such things? Give her a tech puzzle and she could solve it. Ask her to adapt a program, tweak a system, or even build one from scratch and she could do it easily. But emotional stuff? She was lucky if she even realized emotions were involved. Relationships? She'd never had a serious one in her life. Not the kind Brennan and Cash now had, or even her cousin, Sinead. No, she'd had about as much luck as her brother Patrick had had on the relationship front, and had thought herself just as disinterested.

But then she'd met Kyle…

She snapped herself out of useless musings about things that made her feel too much, and went back to the thought she'd had just before falling asleep last night. The possibility she might be right, that what had occurred to her might actually have merit, had her restless. Enough to start pacing again.

She wanted to discuss it with the team, but she couldn't do that until she'd gleaned everything she could in support of it. And she couldn't do that until she talked to Kyle. For all she knew, his answer to her question could refute her theory completely.

Plus she had to decide how much to tell the team— her brothers—about her situation here. So far she'd kept it to a minimum, just saying she'd found Xander's half brother and things were more complicated than she'd expected, because his father—and Xander's—had just been let out of prison early. But she hadn't mentioned, yet anyway, the specific threat to her. Because she knew her brothers, and that protect their little sister gene was going to kick into high gear if she did. And their zeal to protect her could affect the case.

She kept pacing. Thinking. But it always came back to the same thing. What she would do next would depend on Kyle's answer to the question she had yet to ask.

...he hated that guy, too. Even more than our father, I think. Or at least...more viciously. Wished him gone more than once.

Kyle's words about Xander's stepfather ran through her mind once more. Could it be that simple, that basic?

She was so worked up about it that it burst from her the moment he stepped back inside, before he even had a chance to take off the jacket that was indeed dusted with snow.

"Did you ever meet or at least see Xander's stepfather?"

His brow furrowed at the unexpected question and he finished pulling off the jacket before he answered her. "C.J.? Yeah, I saw him a couple of times."

"How old was he then?"

The furrow deepened. "I don't know. I was just a kid, adults all seemed old to me. Maybe...thirties, then? But I heard he died a few years ago. Car crash or something."

She sucked in a deep breath and asked the big question. "What did he look like?"

The furrow deepened. "Kind of average, I guess. Why?"

"Do you remember what color his hair was? His eyes?"

"What—"

She cut him off. "Please, Kyle, this is important."

He let out an audible breath as his gaze went distant

for a moment, as if trying to remember. "Blond hair, I remember that. And I'm pretty sure his eyes were blue."

Male, thirties, blond hair, blue eyes.

The only consistent similarities between all of the Landmark Killer's victims.

It all fit. The faked résumé and background, the abusive stepfather, the victims who resembled that stepfather...

Xander Washer had just shot to the top of the suspect list.

Chapter 29

Kyle refused her suggestion that they sit down. He didn't want to get back on the couch where he'd had all those crazy dreams last night. Dreams of her, lying there with him, cuddled up close, sharing the small space and an amazing amount of warmth. Making him want in ways he never had before.

It had felt so real he'd actually been puzzled for a moment when he'd awakened and she wasn't there. And then he'd been embarrassed, both by the silliness of what he'd dreamed and the fierce sense of loss he felt at realizing that was all it had been, a dream.

So he stayed on his feet, but was so restless he couldn't seem to stay still. He walked over to the fireplace and stirred up the remaining glowing coals, added a couple of sticks of kindling and when they caught added a couple of the smaller logs to get things going.

As he crouched there in front of the fire he couldn't

stop himself from looking through the double-sided fireplace that served to warm both living room and bedroom. The bedroom she was using. And he saw with a little jolt that the bed in that room was undisturbed. It was as tidily made up as it had been when they'd arrived here at the cabin. As if no one had been in it at all last night.

As if the occupant had spent the night somewhere else.

Idiot. She made the freaking bed when she got up, that's all. Quit looking for ways those dreams were true.

Finally he pivoted and sat on the raised hearth, facing her but a safe distance between them. Inwardly he braced himself. He might not be the best at reading human reactions—horses, yes, people no—but he had no doubt that his answer to her odd question about Xander's stepfather had been what she'd somehow expected.

Or feared.

"You going to explain, or are you going to hide behind all that alphabet agency stuff?"

"I need to give you some history, first."

"One of my favorite subjects." He'd had enough of secrets, and didn't even try to keep the sarcasm out of his voice. She winced slightly, and he felt a spark of guilt, but quashed it.

"First of all, you have to realize this isn't proof," she cautioned. "Only stronger suspicion."

"Y'all are always covering your…backside, aren't you?" he drawled out, feeling his tension vibrating just below the surface.

"You know about the Landmark Killer," she began.

"Sometimes I think you guys pick out those names to make yourselves look good."

She didn't wince this time. She must have braced herself. And he tried to ignore that he didn't like being the one who made her feel under attack. "You can thank the media for this one."

"Thank the media? Not likely."

He couldn't seem to stop with the jabs. But she ignored it again. "It fits, in this case. Every one of the victims worked at a well-known landmark in the city, and the media realized that and ran with it."

"So what, the killer is just randomly picking out guys who work at famous places?"

"Not randomly." She took in a deep breath. "He has a fixation on a woman named Maeve O'Leary, a black widow—you know the term?"

"Woman who marries men and then kills them, right?"

She nodded. "In her case rich men, although we don't think that's a factor in the Landmark case, these victims weren't wealthy. She's in prison now. And the Landmark Killer's goal, as he states it in his communications, is to see her freed. So he's picking his victims by their first names. With their initials spelling out Maeve O'Leary."

He stared at her, all other thoughts blasted out of his head by the twisted perversity of what she was telling him. "He's spelling out her name...by killing people?"

She nodded. "He's finished her first name. Now he says he's starting on her last, *O* is up next."

His stomach churned fiercely. "What kind of...person could even think of that?"

"Our profiler laid it out. The killer is an obviously deeply troubled young man, triggered by a father figure from his past. We think his fascination with O'Leary is because he wishes his own mother would have done the same thing to that father figure that she did to her husbands."

"So this is his twisted idea of…what, a tribute?"

"Yes. And he's gotten the idea that she'll be released just to stop him. But we also think it's directly connected to that father figure. That it's his way of taking the revenge he never did back then."

He was feeling an awful combination of stunned and sick. But through that it finally hit him, and he put it together with her urgent question. And asked, a bit unsteadily, "The people he's killing, by their initials… they're all blond with blue eyes, aren't they?"

She didn't try to cushion it. "Yes."

He couldn't describe the horror that filled him. He felt as if his brain were racing wildly, looking for an escape hatch. He grabbed the only thing that occurred to him.

"But why not our father?" he finally blurted out. "If anybody deserves it, he does."

"But your biological father wasn't around to abuse him on a daily basis," she said. "And you have to realize, people who become serial killers are…wired differently. Your father may be a killer, but he didn't kill anyone Xander cared about. If indeed he cares about anyone."

"Except that black widow?"

"Yes. And he only cares about her because she did what he wished his mother had done."

He went quiet for a long moment, trying to slow the chaos of his thoughts. It just seemed so impossible, and yet…how could he really deny it was true? He'd already admitted to her he barely knew his half brother. Certainly not well enough to categorically state he couldn't be this kind of person.

Xander, a serial killer…

No, he couldn't with confidence say it was impossible. Not when during what little time he had spent with him, he'd always been angry. Sometimes overtly, sometimes showing only in his eyes. Eyes that, Kyle realized now, had more than once glinted with an expression that had made him edgy to even be around him.

It wasn't impossible. In fact, it was very possible. Despite her caution that this was not yet proof he could sense she was nearly convinced that it was true.

Nausea rose again. He suppressed a shudder. He knew his father was a killer. Now he knew his half brother could very well be a serial killer. How was he supposed to deal with that?

His head began to throb. His fingers dug into his temples, and he wished he could dig them into his brain and stop the thoughts, rip out the knowledge he now had.

He buried his face in his hands.

Ashlynn hated the look that had come over him, as if he were physically ill. She was sure that was how he felt. She certainly would. And she hated that she'd been the one to do this to him, to swamp him with this awful reality. Because while she knew they didn't have all the evidence they needed, she was convinced now this was the right track.

Ordinarily, that would be her complete focus. She would be up to her neck in this case, never stopping until she'd found what they needed, actual evidence. She might be seventy-five percent sure she was on the right track, but that missing twenty-five percent had tripped up more than one case.

But she couldn't walk away, not when she'd just dumped this truckload of horror on this man who'd done nothing but be born to a killer, and had just found out he might be brother to an even worse killer. This man who'd done nothing except be nice to her.

This man who stirred her like no other ever had.

And for the first time since she'd gone to work for the team, she put that work second. She went over and sat beside Kyle, putting an arm around him. He stiffened, but didn't pull away. In fact, she thought maybe he might have leaned into her a little.

"I'm sorry, Kyle. I'm so very sorry. I hate that you have to deal with this. You must feel as if you just got hit by a truck."

"More like a runaway train," he muttered. After a long moment he gave her a sideways look. "Dump things like this on people often, do you?"

She shook her head. "Never. I'm never out in the field. I rarely even meet the people involved in our cases." Her mouth twisted wryly. "If I was, I probably would have handled this better. So I'm doubly sorry."

He let out a short, sharp breath. "I don't think there is a way to handle something like this better."

"I should have figured out a way so you never even wondered if...you might be like them. Because you're not, Kyle. You're not."

She hadn't even tried to keep the emotion out of her voice or her distress out of her expression, and she knew by the way he kept looking at her that he'd both heard and seen.

"So what happens now?"

"I need to update my team. But it can wait a little longer."

He lapsed into silence for a long moment, a silence that seemed to claw at her, as if there was now something inside her that simply had to know what he was thinking, or at the least that he was all right.

When he finally spoke again, it was the last thing she'd expected.

"Did you stay last night? With me?"

Her breath caught. Her gaze flicked over to the couch where she had indeed spent the night. With him.

"I…yes. I fell asleep, so soundly, for the first time since this started…"

"I thought I'd dreamed it."

She felt heat rise to her cheeks; she'd had a couple of rather…potent dreams herself last night.

"Ashlynn," he said, and stopped. But then he leaned toward her, his gaze fixed on her face. His head tilted slightly, and she heard his breathing quicken. Realized with a little shock what was happening.

He was going to kiss her.

Her mind shouted, "At last!" and it didn't matter at all that it had been less than a week. But then he hesitated, even as he was so close to her. All she could think was that she didn't want him to stop, and so she closed the tiny space between them herself. And the moment their lips touched, she knew they'd sparked something momentous.

And there was no turning back.

Chapter 30

Kyle wasn't sure which hit him harder, that she, in the end, had moved in for the kiss, or the wave of heat that shimmered through him at the feel of her mouth on his. She woke up every nerve ending he had, setting them tingling, until he felt as if he were standing in the open during a fierce thunderstorm, with lightning striking far too close.

When she stroked his lips with her tongue he groaned and deepened the kiss, because he couldn't not. His hands came up to cup her face, to hold her in place while he pressed deeper for more. She tasted like nothing he'd ever had before, like some exotic, impossibly sweet delicacy he couldn't afford.

Couldn't afford.

The truth of that chilled him as nothing else could have. He broke the kiss. The tiny sound of protest she made almost drew him back, but he hung on to what little bit of sanity he had left and pulled back.

He stood up suddenly, knowing that if he didn't step away from her he'd weaken and end up in a bigger vat of misery than he was already in.

"Kyle?"

There was a tremulous note in her voice that was like a knife to his gut. She sounded like she wanted him to take that step back, like she didn't understand why he'd left her, after that kiss.

No choice, no choice...

He mentally repeated it like a mantra, or a vow he had to keep reminding himself of. Because no matter how much he might want to go back for more, he didn't dare. There was no future to this. And that that was an issue was his own fault, he knew. Because he'd never been able to quash an innate desire for something more, more than the occasional hookup.

He didn't want to be his father, moving from woman to woman. Or leaving the occasional essentially father-less kid in his wake.

He smothered a sigh. His mother had told him once, when he'd pressed, that she and his father had only married because she wouldn't sleep with him other-wise. Kyle had always had the feeling this had been a novelty to Victor, interesting enough to make him do it. Not that it had kept him around, of course.

A memory, harsh and sharp, hit him. That day he'd come home early because of a power failure at school, and found them arguing. He'd been trying to sneak to his room unheard and unseen, but their rented house was so tiny he knew he wouldn't be able to. So he'd frozen there out of sight in the entry, while they shouted in the kitchen.

He'd gotten there just as his mother shouted, "I gave you a son!"

And stayed just long enough to hear his father answer just as loudly, "Already had one of those, didn't want that one or this one!"

In shock Kyle had backed up the way he'd come, out of the house, to go hide in his refuge, the small tool shed in the back yard. It was safe there; it wasn't like his father ever actually used any of the various maintenance tools that were stored there by the landlord.

The shock hadn't been at the declaration his father hadn't wanted him, he'd known that, thought he always had.

The shock had been the knowledge that there was another son out there. He'd never known. And later, when Victor had left on one of his binges, he'd confronted his mother about what he'd heard, only to find she'd known all along, and that it was why she'd insisted on marriage first; she didn't want to be a single mother with no legal claim.

For all the good that did her. He had nothing to claim in the first place.

"Kyle," Ashlynn said again. softly, snapping him out of the pointless contemplation he hadn't indulged in in years.

"Don't you need to make that…notification, or report, or whatever it is you're supposed to do?"

"But you—"

"Just do what you need to do," he said, hating that it was coming out through clenched teeth.

"Instead of what I want, you mean?"

He didn't look at her. He didn't dare. Because he knew what he'd see in those eyes of hers, the heat of that kiss. She wasn't thinking clearly, that had to be it. So he had to do it for both of them.

"Ashlynn, please. I…need a minute." Or longer, maybe a lot longer, to tamp things down. In particular his body's response to that kiss. It had been like wildfire, erupting suddenly, and almost immediately out of control.

"Fine," she finally said. "But don't think this is over."

I didn't want it to be over. I wanted it to be just the beginning.

The admission ripped through his mind as he watched her walk away, back to her computer setup. It wasn't far enough. He headed for the bathroom, thinking that dunking his head in that shiveringly cold water that had made her yelp before might solve his problem.

But then that other memory, from that bathroom, rose up to slice that idea to ribbons.

Did you stay last night? With me?

I…yes.

He closed the door behind him, letting out a strangled, bitter laugh. Not even a shower under that icy water was going to solve this problem.

It took Ashlynn several starts and stops and a thorough proofread before her text was ready to send. She was glad she had the program on her laptop, because it would have been a mess had she had to do it all on her phone. Well, the team's phone, since her personal phone was temporarily dead and locked up back at the office so there was no way the killer—she wasn't ready to substitute Xander's name, not yet—could track her with it.

Laying it all out for them, that Xander had had a stepfather he'd hated whose description matched the victims, and that he had "wished him gone," made it even harder to rein in her suspicions that Xander was indeed their killer.

She hesitated about adding the next bit, because it felt a bit like betraying Kyle, and it was a tenuous connection anyway. But they needed to know everything, if they were going to stop this killer, so for the sake of the victims to come, she went ahead with the information that Xander's father had murdered his half brother's girlfriend.

She still had not told them Victor had directly threatened her, because she knew it would mess up their focus and they needed to be zeroed in on the Landmark Killer now. Besides, then she'd have to explain why, and she didn't want to trigger that radar. Not when the fact that the entire team except her and Patrick had ended up with their personal lives beautifully settled in the last few months. So she had merely told them she was taking precautions since Victor had been released early and had been seen at the ranch, watching Kyle.

Nor had she told them about the thing that had popped up in her searching this morning. There were valid reasons for Xander to have a second personal peer-to-peer payment account—she knew many at the agency did, to separate business and personal payments—and until she had a chance to dig into it more, she didn't want to toss unnecessary speculation into the mix. It was her job to determine if it meant anything, and she hadn't yet.

She sent the message. As she'd expected, it took only a few minutes after she got the notification that it had been delivered for an answer to come back. This one came from Brennan's phone.

Good job. We'll be going over the latest as soon as Cash gets here. Watch your back.

I am. Any developments?

No. We're so close, but we still need something concrete, not just speculation.

I know. Still working on finding that.

There was a pause before another response came in, this one from her cousin, Sinead, the profiler. We may need to consider the possibility Suspect 1 could show up there.

That hadn't occurred to her yet. She answered quickly. I'll ask the brother—what an impersonal way to refer to him—but I'm doubtful.

They wound up the brief chat as Cash arrived, and for a moment Ashlynn just sat there thinking. Her gaze had turned inward, so while she was still in front of the screen showing the sign-off, she wasn't really seeing it.

She was trying to figure out how to approach what she had to ask. How did she dive right back into talking about the case where his brother was a prime suspect after...that kiss?

She had been so focused on the team contact that she hadn't really registered that he'd come back into the room until he came over to the windows to her right and stood there, looking outside.

"Maybe you shouldn't do that," she said awkwardly.

"You make a good target standing there in plain sight like that."

He gave her a sideways look. It was steady enough, with no sign of the turmoil she'd seen in his eyes after that kiss. "Did you forget you are the target, not me?"

Something in his too-level tone jabbed at her. How could he sound like that, so…dispassionate, after that kiss? Her words came out with an edge. "Believe me, I haven't forgotten. But I also know killers can be unpredictable. My cousin, Sinead, could tell you that."

"That's the profiler?"

She was a little surprised he remembered her name. "Yes." She nodded toward the screen, then said, "She brought up something I hadn't thought of."

"I thought you thought of everything."

There wasn't a trace of sarcasm in his voice. But there wasn't a trace of any emotion at all in his voice. It was as if that kiss—weird how she kept thinking about it that way, in those words—hadn't happened at all. She tried for the same kind of tone, keeping it all business for the question she had to ask.

"Do you think your father being released would bring Xander back here? I'm sure he must know, he has access to a lot of databases, and the knowledge to use them."

His brow furrowed in thought. No matter how he was feeling about what had happened between them—she was *not* going to use those two words again—he was thankfully taking this seriously.

"No. No, I don't think he'd come back. He hated it here. All he ever wanted was to be away from here, to leave this life behind and…reinvent himself. I doubt he keeps in touch with anyone from here. Certainly not me." He grimaced. "I wouldn't be surprised if he didn't even know what our father did, that he was in prison at all or why, he cut himself off so completely."

"Well, that's comforting, in a way."

His mouth twisted even further. "I don't know. Maybe I should wish he would come back, because if he is that killer, he might take the old man out and solve all my problems."

That in a nutshell summation left her speechless for a moment. What it must feel like to be in the position where your father killing your half brother is a solution? She couldn't even imagine. And judging by the look in his eyes, he knew just how twisted it was, how out of whack his life had become through no fault of his own.

She made a firm mental note to hug and thank every member of her family when she got back home.

Chapter 31

The snow had stopped a few hours after it had started, leaving only an inch or so on the ground now, three days later. But Kyle still had to stomp his feet on the porch to get it off his boots. Then he brushed off the left shoulder of his jacket, where a branch he'd brushed had dropped its collection of snow onto him, then tapped his hat against his leg a couple of times to make sure it, too, was clear.

This check of the perimeter he'd mentally set had once more turned up nothing suspicious. Not a single sign there was anything or anyone with less than four legs in the vicinity. Maybe the old man had given up. Maybe he'd decided he wasn't worth it.

He closed his eyes as his father's threats came back to him in a rush that was like a punch to the gut.

After what you took from me, you think I'm going to let you just live and be happy?

I'll spend the rest of that life making sure you spend yours alone.

It was funny, in a dark sort of way. Because after Sarah he'd always figured he'd end up alone, had accepted it, so that hadn't seemed like a particularly effective threat. It was only putting Ashlynn—or as his father thought, Zoe—in peril that had gotten to him. He already felt bad enough about Sarah, he didn't want anything added to that load.

Which is why you need to keep your distance from Ashlynn. No matter how damned good that kiss felt.

His resolve renewed, he opened the door and stepped inside. It was nicely warm compared to the chill outside. Before he even started to take off his jacket he looked toward the desk. But she wasn't there. For the first time, she wasn't there, typing away, glued to that screen. She would be no good at it at all, she'd told him, or she'd offer to do some of those outside checks herself. He'd assured her she didn't need to, silently acknowledging he needed the illusion of doing something, anything, even if it was only that, an illusion.

But she wasn't far away. He spotted her the moment he started to look around the room, half sitting, half lying on the far end of the couch, her legs tucked up beside her as she rested her chin on her crossed arms on the arm of the couch. She was staring into the fire, as if she hoped to find answers there she hadn't found on that screen. He thought of these last nights they'd spent here, usually starting in a pleasant silence as she studied things on her laptop and he read. It was an easy sort of silence—as long as he didn't think about that kiss.

But they'd talked, too, him about how much he loved this place and this life and why, her about how much she loved the city, despite the fact that it felt overwhelming sometimes. That was a good thing, for him, because he reminded him that he had no business thinking there might be something left for them when this was over.

He shed the damp jacket and hat and hung them on the rack by the door, then toed off his worn, now damp boots. She looked over at the sound.

"Everything out there all right?"

He nodded. "Are you?"

She gave him a wry smile. "Mostly. Just thinking about the irony of it all."

"Irony?"

"Of coming here to escape one killer only to run right into another."

He walked over quietly in sock-clad feet, and sat on the edge of the big coffee table opposite her. She turned in her seat, sitting upright now. Which he admitted he regretted. For some reason the sight of her so relaxed had made him feel…good. And he almost didn't ask about what had occurred to him, but decided he needed to know if he was going to keep her safe.

"How did you get in his crosshairs? I thought he was targeting a certain type of man?"

To his surprised, her cheeks pinkened a little. "I… ticked him off."

He blinked. "What?"

She explained about a taunting text she'd gotten from the serial killer, and her impulsive response to it. "Stupid, I know, but…it was just a gut reaction. He made me so angry."

She seemed calm enough now, so he risked saying, his voice carefully neutral, "And you're not even a redhead."

She looked startled for an instant, then her expression shifted to rueful. "Okay, I had that one coming."

"Indubitably."

"You know, you don't talk like I ever thought a cowboy would."

He raised a brow at her. "A bit biased, are you?"

"Apparently," she admitted.

"Well, now," he intentionally drawled out, "I could just slide on into your preconceptions and prejudices, ma'am, and drawl my way from here to Houston, if'n that'd make ya more comfortable."

She laughed. "You didn't say y'all."

"That's because there's only one of you." *And that's true in more ways than one.*

"So only say it if there's more than one person. Duly noted," she said, still smiling.

"And simple. It's only when there's a crowd it gets tricky."

"A crowd?"

"Seems nobody can agree on exactly what number makes it go from y'all to all y'all."

She laughed again. "I can see I have a lot to learn."

"Mostly that y'all ain't used up north much."

"Then how do you know all the details?"

"Because the occasional Texan has wandered through, and they cut a wide path."

She chuckled. He was liking that he was making her smile, and even laugh. He was liking it a lot. In fact, more than he could remember liking just about anything lately.

"Speaking of wandering," she said after a moment, "you seem to have a serious case of wanderlust. Why?"

Some kind of lust, anyway.

He yanked his mind off that path, fast. Focused on what she was actually saying.

"I…" His voice almost immediately trailed off, because this wasn't something he talked about. Maybe because he wasn't sure what the answer was anymore. Finally, he went on. "I started out moving a lot because there was no reason to stay and a lot I wanted to leave behind. After a while there was nothing left holding me anywhere."

"I can see why you'd want to leave the painful memories behind," she said.

His mouth twisted. "Yeah. Except it doesn't work that way. Those memories came along as sure as if I'd packed them up in my saddlebags. I'll never be rid of them."

"I know," she said quietly. And he suddenly remembered what she'd said that first day.

"You would know," he said, just as quietly. "Your dad." She nodded. He hesitated, then asked, "What happened?"

She hesitated a moment in turn before saying, even more quietly, "He was a police officer. A very good one. He was killed on duty. Murdered."

His breath jammed up in his throat. She really did understand. And he had the thought that he'd just gotten the explanation for her path in life. Her father had been murdered, so now she helped put murderers away.

While you just run away. Time after time.

"Damn," he muttered. "I'm sorry."

"It's been a long time, now. But those memories are still there and always will be." She gave him a small smile he thought might be the bravest thing he'd ever seen. "Saddlebags or no."

He shook his head, marveling at her. "What kind of

what kind of world is it when good guys like your dad die, and ones like mine are still around? Still alive, to do more damage?"

"It's a hard lesson to learn, that the world isn't fair," she said. Then, her head tilted slightly in that way she had, she asked, "Is that why you keep moving? Your father?"

"It was. Now…now I think it's just something I do." He drew in a deep breath, then gave her what he'd barely admitted to himself. "But the urge has…eased up a lot. It's time for me to go soon, but they're really good people—" he gestured at the cabin they'd been loaned "—obviously, and I like working here."

"So maybe you'll stay?"

"Thinking about it. Feels strange, to even say it. I'm so used to always moving on, and I'm not sure what's changed."

"Maybe it's not the place, or the job that's changed. Maybe it's you."

Now, that was a possibility he hadn't really thought about. That the shift wasn't in the location or the people, but in him. But then the reality of his life crashed back in on him.

"Doesn't matter. I can't stay. He's seen to that. Again."

"What about later? After this is…over?"

He welcomed the needed reminder that this would end, and likely sooner rather than later. The FBI would catch their man—damn, Xander!—and she would go back home to the big city. Safely out of his old man's reach.

He said, as casually as he could. "Then I move on, and have a little bit of peace until he finds me again."

And this time a place where there won't be any smart, cute, sexy women coming through.

"And where will you go?" she asked, sounding worried. As if she really cared where he went, where his pitiful life took him.

With an effort, he quipped. "Don't know. As usual, wherever there's a good library."

A brief smile flitted across her face, but she was shaking her head. "You can't go on like that forever, Kyle."

He'd known he was close to hitting the wall with these emotions he wasn't used to feeling, but now he slammed into it.

"What am I supposed to do? Now that he's out, he'll follow me, haunt me, and probably kill anyone he thinks is close to me, whether it's true or not. Ashlynn, he wants to kill *you*, because he thinks...he thinks..."

He couldn't finish it. Couldn't repeat the foolishness that his father wanted to kill her because he thought they were in a relationship.

Thought they were in love.

She moved suddenly, and in the next second was sitting beside him on the coffee table, her arms around him. She murmured his name, softly, and he broke, turning to her and returning the hug, the holding.

"You know what I think?" she whispered.

"Rarely," he said, thinking that this woman would be a lifetime challenge for the man lucky enough to win her.

She smiled, and a delightful shiver went through him. "I think—" her arms tightened around him "—if we're going to get murdered for it anyway, we might as well enjoy it."

He looked down at her in shock. Saw an impossible warmth and longing in those rich brown eyes.

And then she kissed him.

Chapter 32

She felt his moment of frozen hesitation. As if he were shocked that she'd done it. He shouldn't be, she'd done this before. Which in itself was odd, she wasn't the type who began things very often. Or in fact, ever. Yet she'd initiated a kiss with him twice.

And hoped that now she'd initiated even more.

She understood his hesitancy. She was still a guest where he worked, and she supposed there were rules about getting involved with clients. But they weren't back at the main ranch, where they would be noticed. They were alone, isolated, and for now at least it seemed, safe.

Safe.

She'd heard field agents joking about adrenaline surges, and how they kicked other urges into high gear. Maybe it was true. Maybe this was just her reaction to the jolt of realizing she was a target. Maybe this was a case of wanting some hot sex before she maybe got killed. She didn't really care at this point, not when every nerve in her body was taut and ready, making her ache for any sign she wasn't alone in this.

And then he was kissing her back, fiercely, with an urgency that matched her own. Whatever she was feeling, he was feeling it too, and that only added fuel to the fire that was rippling through her. The sensation of his mouth on hers made her lips part. Before she could do what she wanted to, taste him long and deep, he did it first. The touch of his tongue, seeking, probing, turned that fire into an inferno, and she clutched at him.

He broke the kiss.

A little cry of protest escaped her before she could stop it. She would have been devastated had she not heard the rapid pant of his breathing.

"Ash," he murmured between breaths. "Don't start this if you don't mean to finish it."

Relief flooded her. Because that was exactly what she wanted. Not the finish, but the journey to that finish was something she wanted in ways she'd never known before. Ways that made the nickname she'd never liked sound beautiful to her, when it came from him, in that rough, low voice.

"Oh, I mean to," she whispered. "And I can be pretty stubborn."

To her pleasant surprise, she heard a low chuckle. "I noticed."

And she realized suddenly that was one of the reasons she was here, now, wanting him like this.

He noticed.

Big things, little things, he noticed.

"Want to know what I noticed?"

"Besides the fact that you're driving me crazy?"

She smiled, and it echoed in her voice when she said, "I noticed that this place truly is fully stocked."

He blinked, clearly puzzled.

"There's a box of condoms in the nightstand."

He smiled back at her then, and everything she'd ever wanted to hear in his voice was there when he arched a brow at her and said, "Only one?"

She laughed and then she was in his arms and it felt more right than anything ever had. And what she had expected would be swift, half-crazed, was instead a slow, sinuous, flowing thing that didn't explode but blossomed as he slowly touched her, stroked her and kissed her as if she were some deliciously exotic thing he'd never tasted before. She wanted him to hurry but he wouldn't, and it was driving her mad.

At least, it had seemed as if he wasn't hurrying but here they were, in the bedroom, clothes already half off. He was even more beautiful than she'd expected, with that body honed into powerful definition not by hours in a gym but simple hard work. As they went down to the bed she ran her hands over his arms, savoring the strength in them, his chest, savoring the broadness of it, then the rippling muscles of his abs. When she couldn't resist moving further, she felt his belly contract as he sucked in an audible breath.

And then he began to move, his hands tracing her as if he wanted to memorize every curve, every line of her. His fingers were like fire trailing along her skin, and when he began to follow the same paths with his mouth she gasped as the fire became a blaze. He cupped her breasts, teased her nipples until she couldn't hold still. Then he replaced those delightfully work-rough-ened fingers with his mouth and she moaned, unable to stop herself. She arched up to him, her fingers curling around male flesh that was clearly ready. When he let out a low groan it kicked her pulse into high gear as she relished the simple fact that giving him pleasure doubled her own. She'd never been so revved up so fast. And somehow she found a way, with caresses and some murmured urgings, to let him know that.

After a moment's wrestling with the condom he came back to her. Then, in the moment before it would have been too late to ask, he said in a voice so rough it sent another kind of heat through her, "You're sure, Ash? Absolutely sure?"

"I'm sure that if I don't have you in the next second I'm going to go stark, raving—"

He cut off her words, making her gasp as he started to move. She'd already known how close she was so it was no surprise to her that she was slick enough that he slid into her easily. Yet he stretched her, filled her, so perfectly she cried out at the incredible sensation of it. And when he whispered to her, when he called her "Ash" again, she decided she loved the shortened version of her name after all.

And when she heard it again, bursting from him in the same moment his name broke from her as her body clenched around him, she knew she wanted to hear it from him forever.

Much later, in the quiet darkness, she lay with his arms around her, reveling in what she'd learned about love and her herself in the last few hours.

She didn't regret it. She couldn't quite believe she'd done it, initiated it, but how could she regret it? How could she, when she'd never felt better in her life? She snuggled up to his warmth, almost laughing inwardly at the memory of her few other experiences that had left her thinking, *This is it?*

How many times had she wondered if this was truly all there was to that most physical of connections? Pleasant, but hardly consuming. Yet she had looked at Brennan, at Cash, at her cousin, Sinead, and they seemed... transcendent now that they'd found that one person they seemed to be meant for. She'd begun to wonder if there was something wrong with her, that she didn't experience what they seemed to.

And now she understood. This was what it was supposed to be like. This crazy, heart-melting, body-soaring meeting of two people. She even—her cheeks flushed anew—screamed last night. But the pressure he'd built inside her with every stroke of his muscled body had simply reached a point where she had to let it out somehow or explode, so the scream of his name had come out.

And then she'd exploded anyway.

Maybe it was simply that she'd never been certain before that a man wanted her. Not just sex, not just the release, but *her*. But Kyle had left her no doubts.

No doubts.

Well, not about that. The doubts were there, hovering, about where this might go from here, if anywhere, but she wasn't going to think about that now. Eventually, when they had to confront reality again, when they had to face the simple fact of how utterly incompatible their lives were...

But not now.

He stirred beside her. Made a sound almost like a sigh. Then, suddenly, he went rigidly still. And slowly, very slowly, opened his eyes. Those rich, warm brown eyes she practically drowned in last night.

"It was real."

She could barely hear the words, he whispered them so quietly, as if he hadn't meant to say them aloud at all. But the wonder in his barely audible tone washed over her, and she realized he thought he'd dreamed what had happened between them.

Did that mean he'd...dreamed about them before? Together, as they had been last night, as they were now.

She couldn't stop the smile that curved her mouth at just the thought.

"Oh, it was real. The most real, the most wonderful thing of my life," she said softly.

He reached for her then, and that quickly the blaze was kindled again. She felt the thrill rising in her again, that incredible feeling of being this for someone. As he'd murmured into the darkness, the desire he'd never expected to feel, the treasure he'd never expected to find.

It was much later, as they lay entwined, that he said, "Don't regret this. Crazy as this is, please don't regret it. I know I'm the guy who was too blind to believe my father would do what he'd said he would, but—"

"And I'm the woman who spent more time with Xander than it seems you ever did, but never suspected him."

He propped himself up on one elbow to look at her. "I didn't think of it like that. So...we're both blind?"

She studied him for a moment, saw the shadows stirring in his eyes, a trace of that haunted look she'd hoped was banished.

"Maybe, even though we'd have every right with my work and your life, we haven't quite gotten to where we always expect the worst in people."

"I don't want to live there," he said, his voice tight.

"Then we won't," she said, putting a little emphasis on the *we*.

She lifted a hand and stroked his cheek, thrilling anew at the way his eyes drifted half-closed, as if he were savoring even this slight touch. And in that moment she quashed, for now at least, the thoughts in the back of her mind about how utterly different their lives were, how far apart their realities were, and how the city girl and the country boy might be combustible together, but could it be anything more than that?

She didn't let herself wonder if there was any kind of future for them, because she didn't want to think about the very real possibility there wasn't one. So instead, when he reached out for her she went gladly, eager to once more hear her name, sounding as if it had been ripped out of him by a pleasure as great as her own.

Chapter 33

As he made his check of the perimeter he'd mentally set, Kyle found he had to force himself to stay alert and on task. There had been no sign of Victor since they'd gotten here, and despite his self-warnings not to be lulled or yet again underestimate his father's capacity for evil, his mind kept wanting to wander to what felt like the biggest question he was facing. Which was silly given the circumstances. But there it was, hovering.

If this past week—and the last three nights they'd spent together in bed, kindling a fire that burned even hotter than the one on the open hearth—hadn't been crazy enough here he was having to stop himself from imagining a future with Ashlynn Colton in it. Their lives couldn't be more different, more...uncombinable.

As he turned to start back to the cabin, he stopped dead in his tracks at what he saw. The big front windows—until now thought of mostly as a hazard, given the view they gave—showing him the front room, fire casting light and a warmth he would welcome getting back to, but most of all Ash.

The threat the open view caused vanished for a moment, erased by the sheer pleasure of just looking at her as this amazing woman did what she did, used that clearly prodigious brain of hers toward keeping people safe from people like this Landmark Killer.

Who could be Xander. Your father could have passed it on, that twisted lizard brain thing.

His mind wanted to jump into the fray, wondering yet again if it had been passed on to him as well, but Ash's certainty about that soothed the qualms. She would know, wouldn't she? It was her job, after all.

And she already knows you better than anyone ever has.

He felt a qualm at that thought, remembering Sarah, but they'd been so young, so naive. Maybe they would have reached this point eventually, but now, with Ash... had it really been only ten days?

She was deep into her research when he made it back inside, so he took care to be as quiet as he could. He wanted to go to her, to lean over and kiss the back of her neck, sweep his tongue over that delicate ear in the way he'd learned made her shiver, but...she had a serial killer to help catch.

He was ensconced in his favorite spot for reading—although he had to admit he spent more time watching her—when he heard her sudden, sharp intake of breath. And while she was always intent when working, this somehow felt different. Not just intent but...intense.

Her fingers began to fly on the keys and the screen changed so rapidly he couldn't imagine how she could be seeing or reading what was on it. It went from a document with columns to a photograph of something on a city street to a map image. Then she backed it up to the document, as if to double-check. Then back to the map.

Finally, she took a long deep breath and leaned back in the chair. And he heard her whisper a heartfelt oath.

"Ash? You all right?"

She spun around in the chair, not as if she were surprised he was there, but decisively.

"I am very all right," she said, and he caught a gleam of excitement in her rich brown eyes. But as she focused on him the gleam faded, to be replaced by a look of concern and a furrow in her brow. "But…"

"But what?"

"You may not be."

It took him a moment to make the jump. When he did, he felt his stomach knot. "You found something. On Xander."

She hesitated, then nodded.

His jaw tightened. He relaxed it and asked, "What did you find?" When she didn't answer, he had the thought that maybe she couldn't. "Let me guess, you can't talk about it?"

"I shouldn't, but…" She let out an audible sigh. "I can't keep it secret, either. Not from you."

He supposed it was ridiculous that he zeroed in on that "not from you" more than anything else, but he couldn't seem to help it. Since he was certain if he tried to speak something stupid would come out, he just waited. She took another deep breath and then spoke.

"A while ago I found that Xander had two payment app accounts. One linked to his bank account, the other a cash balance only, funded by a large deposit made early this year. There's nothing unusual about that in itself, but…the second one was under the last name Slater."

Kyle's brow furrowed. "He never used the old man's name."

"That's what I thought. That maybe it was coincidence, despite the unlikelihood of there being two Xander Slaters. But when I backtracked far enough I found that Xander—the one we know as Xander Washer—made a withdrawal from his personal bank account, in cash, in the exact amount that opened the payment account. And on the same day."

"A few too many coincidences." His stomach was knotting tighter. Then, his brow furrowing again, he asked, "But you said you found this out a while ago… What did you find out just now?"

One corner of her mouth—that mouth he'd now tasted so thoroughly—lifted in a half smile. At what? That he'd remembered what she'd said? Hell, he remembered every damned thing she'd said to him since he'd looked up from grooming Splash and seen her face.

"I found a receipt from his original account from a Starbucks on 88th Street in the city, near where he lives on the Upper West Side, time-stamped early in the morning. The same morning our second victim was murdered at the Empire State Building."

"Pardon my ignorance of New York City's geography, but what does that tell you?"

She gave him a slight smile again. "Sorry. We do sometimes tend to assume everybody knows."

"Because you're so famous and all." He managed not to roll his eyes, but it was a close thing.

"Well, the city is," she said reasonably. "Anyway, that

Starbucks is more than fifty blocks away from the scene of the second murder, so I didn't think anything of it."

"Until?" he asked quietly.

She sighed. "Until I remembered something. Something I should have remembered sooner. Something that…could put him in the area of the second murder within the range of the estimated time of death."

"Remembered what?"

"We had a team meeting that day, within an hour after word of the second murder came out. Xander was there, and so was I." She hesitated, as if gathering herself for a jump into a pool she couldn't see the bottom of. "He wasn't drinking a Starbucks. He had a cup from another coffee shop."

He blinked. "You remember his coffee cup?"

"Because we joked—I thought—about it. About him carrying supporting local businesses a little far."

"So what does that prove?" He was totally puzzled now.

Something in her gaze changed then, and he knew she was about to hit him with it. "I found the payment record on that second account under the alias. The shop where he bought that coffee isn't a chain, it's an indie business." She took the deepest breath yet and plunged ahead. "There's only one of them. And it's two blocks from the Empire State Building."

Ashlynn waited, almost holding her breath. Almost hoping Kyle would say something that would blow her theory out of the water, make it impossible that his half brother really was the Landmark Killer.

He was on his feet now, looking around the room as if the answer was hiding there somehow. Then he was moving, in that sudden-start kind of way that she was all too-familiar with, that moment when it becomes simply impossible to stay still because of what was boiling up in your mind.

The surprising part was that the dread she was feeling wasn't about finding out her supposed friend was quite possibly the murderer they sought, but that it was Kyle's brother. She couldn't fathom what he must be going through, first his father and now this.

Finally he came to a halt beside her. She stood up, because she felt she had to. In a low, harsh voice, he said, "It's him, isn't it? It's really true."

She wanted to say something soothing, something calming, but she couldn't, wouldn't lie to him. Not again. "It's looking that way."

She didn't add what she was thinking, that Xander had done what serial killers usually do eventually; he'd screwed up.

Or underestimated how stubborn you are.

She had to suppress a shudder at the memory of all the times she'd shared a table with the man at lunch. But then the more she thought about it, the madder she got, thinking about his lighthearted manner, his utter certainty that she would never, ever tumble to the truth.

"You're angry."

His quiet statement startled her. And she answered more readily than she normally would have. And more than she probably should have. "Yes. I am. I'm always angry about serial killers getting away with it. But in this case, I'm extra angry because of what this is putting you through. And because he thinks I'm stupid, blind or both." She paused, took a deep breath to calm down, and then admitted, "And I'm angry because he was pretty much right, for too long."

To her amazement he took that last step between them and put his arms around her. The man had just found out his half brother was likely a serial killer, and his first thought was to comfort her? She went all soft inside; she couldn't think of another way to describe it.

"I think I figured it out," she said softly against his broad, strong chest.

"So it seems. Xander is the killer."

"I don't mean that. I mean you." He went very still. "I think all the good that would have usually been divided up between your father, Xander and you, all went to you instead."

He laughed, and it was a little shaky. "Don't try taking that to the bank."

"Don't want to. I want to keep it."

This time it felt as if he'd even stopped breathing. Too late she realized what it had sounded like, that she wanted to keep…him. She opened her mouth to lighten it up, but no words came. Because, she realized, it was the truth. She couldn't deny it any longer. And the fact that it had been barely over a week since she'd met him didn't matter at all. Nor did the fact that their lives were so disparate, on the surface unblendable.

So we'll dig past the surface. There has to be a way.

Because there was no denying the bottom line, in all its improbability.

She loved him.

Chapter 34

As he paced the floor again Kyle watched her typing out a text detailing her discovery to her team. She paused, as if uncertain of something, then added a final line before sending it. Then, like someone who'd finished an onerous task, she abruptly stood up. And for the first time since she'd set it up, she actually closed the laptop.

"You've told them about the coffee shop?"

She turned to look at him and nodded. "And to be very careful, because… I think it's really him. And he's smart."

"And sneaky," Kyle said sourly.

"Yes. That too." She met his gaze. "I'm sorry, Kyle."

"You're sorry? He's the killer."

"But you're the one who's now looking at both of your male relatives being killers."

He stiffened. "I don't want your pity, Ashlynn."

He saw her react to his reversion to her full name. He hadn't meant to hurt her, but he was stung by the very idea that she felt sorry for him.

"I don't pity you. Sympathy, yes. At least, that's what it was at first, but now…it's more. Because you're more. More than just a person of interest in an investigation to me. So much more."

"Because we had sex?" he asked bluntly, not sure where this urge to hammer at her had come from. She reacted to his tone and the question with an openness and honesty that totally disarmed him.

"Stop it. We would never have had sex if you weren't already more than that to me."

His annoyance shattered and fell away at the total honesty that rang in both her words and her voice.

He swore under his breath. Crossed the short space between them in a single stride. "I'm the one who's sorry, Ash. I just… I don't…"

For a long moment he gave up trying to find words that wouldn't come and simply held her. And she let him, despite his momentary snarkiness. And holding her like that, feeling her acquiescence to being in his arms, drained away his tension. There was nothing left but certainty about two things. One, that he already felt more for this woman than he had anyone in his life, even his dead youthful love. And two, the sudden realization that he was utterly exhausted with his life. He was tired of running, of starting over time after time, searching for something he had never found.

Until now.

Because he had the feeling he'd found it all, all he'd ever wished for and more right here, in the woman he held.

They ended up back in the bedroom, and this time it

was a slow, gentle, aching exploration of each other, a learning of each other, and not just physically. She was even more giving than she had been, although before this Kyle would have said that was impossible.

But the new openness, the removal of all barriers, shattered any illusions he had left that this wasn't what he'd thought it was, and that sometimes how long you've known someone didn't matter. And in the first moments after he slid into her sleek, warm body he had the thought that for this, he'd give up almost anything.

For her.

"When your team catches him…what happens then?"

Ashlynn ran a finger over his ribs as he lay beside her the next morning, wondering if she would ever get tired of seeing the smile that curved his mouth—that mouth that had so recently driven her mad when he'd applied it to every sensitive place on her body, and places she'd never thought of that way—when she touched him. As if he were in complete wonder that she would want to.

"The usual," she said. "Reports to write, evidence to catalog, on and on." *And I, for the first time in maybe ever, felt no urge to leap for my phone or laptop this morning. I'm learning to really like this remote place.*

Or maybe it was just having this man in bed beside her. She had to quash what she was certain would have been a far too satisfied smile.

"I meant you," he said.

"Oh." She spent a brief moment marveling that he could even think about that, when it was his brother they were talking about, and the lethal shadow of their joint father was hovering. "I…guess I go back to work."

He was quiet for a moment, his gaze lowered, long

enough for her to notice again the thick fans of his eyelashes. Then, as if he'd needed that moment to decide what to say, he looked back at her. "Seems to me you never stopped. You've worked every day since you've been here."

She smiled at that. "But not every minute," she pointed out.

She got a full smile for that. And that made her say what was more on her mind at this moment than the Landmark Killer in New York. "At the moment, I'm more worried about your father. Until he's stopped…"

"He hasn't done anything yet but make threats," he said, so tiredly he sounded as if he were contemplating the likelihood of that going on for the rest of his life.

"And violate the terms of his parole by failing to check in with his parole officer. That should be enough to put him right back where he was."

"If they ever catch him."

She refused to contemplate the possibility that he might have to live for years with this hanging over him. "When they do…what will you do?"

Those eyes she loved closed for a moment. And his voice was strangely hollow when he said, "I don't know. I just know I'm…tired. Tired of running, and constantly starting over."

Ashlynn felt an odd tangle of emotions at his words. Pain, for the way he sounded, but also hope, at this first admission that he was weary of this life he'd been leading, always moving on. This first sign that maybe, just maybe, he might be open to a change.

Before her imagination could take off and build a castle in the sky where they both lived happily ever after, she reined it in. But she didn't want to. This was all new to her, this feeling that she'd found something she hadn't really been aware she was searching for.

A sudden memory hit, of that night in her hotel room, when she'd begun the search that had led her here. A memory of what she'd thought as she'd set up that search. *If there was a mention of her particular Kyle Slater anywhere on line, eventually she'd find it...*

Her Kyle Slater.

A shiver of pleasure, a sharp echo of what he caused in her with his touch, went through her.

Her Kyle Slater.

How she wanted that to be true. But did he?

She spent much of that morning trying to decide how to bring it up. How did you initiate a talk about the future with someone who had lived his kind of life? How did someone with his past even think about the future, when he seemed certain his life would just go on endlessly as it had?

By afternoon she was having trouble thinking at all, because there was nothing to help her in the places she usually turned to. Websites, statistics, evidence tracking, none of it helped her with this. Not that she hadn't tried, but all she'd turned up were platitudes and clichés that were too general to be of any use to her.

She stood in front of the windows, looking out. And oddly, for her, she was seized with a need to stop looking, and experience firsthand. She turned around to look for Kyle, who had been inventorying their supplies in the kitchen. She wondered briefly what they would do when things started to run out. That simple thought, the fact that they could not stay here forever, made her even more anxious to figure things out.

She walked over to the small space that managed to

be the perfect size for the two of them. He looked up the moment she got close.

"Are you planning to do another check outside soon?" she asked.

"Right after this," he said, straightening up from the small, under-counter fridge. Then, his expression shifting, he asked quickly, "Did you see something out there?"

"No, no, not that," she assured him quickly. "I just… Can I come with you?"

He looked surprised at first, but then gave her a crooked smile. "Little cabin fever?"

"Not that…" How could it be when she'd been happier here in these last few days than she could remember? "I like it here, but I need some fresh air, to clear my head."

"Plenty of that out there."

He said it as if he completely understood the need, which relieved her. She'd been concerned he might think she wanted to be away from this little place where she'd found such joy with him, when nothing could be further from the truth. She would never have believed it, but what she'd said was the truth. She liked it here. It had taken some adjustment, yes, but she'd come to like the quiet, the peace, the lack of interruptions. And mentally she was already trying to figure out what she could do to hang on to some of that when she…left here.

Because she would, wouldn't she? True, much of her work could be done remotely, but nothing could replace the in-person meetings of the team. And she could never leave her family. That she'd even thought that for a moment stunned her. But such was the effect this place—and this man—had had on her.

She put on her warmest socks and the boots she'd brought. She added a sweater, and Kyle helped her on with her heavy jacket. She figured that was the best she could do, but then Kyle reached into the small wooden trunk beneath the coat rack. He came up with a knitted woolen hat, with earflaps that ended in tassels and handed it to her.

"It's colder up here," he said.

"What about you?"

"This'll do," he said, reaching for the black cowboy hat.

Since she liked him in the iconic style, she didn't even tease him about it. And wondered when she'd become a Western wear aficionado.

About the time you first laid eyes on him.

It barely even registered anymore that he was taking the rifle, settling it over one shoulder by the attached sling. In fact, she was glad, because his father aside, who knew what might be out there?

She was glad of the hat the moment she stepped outside and the chill hit her. But at the same time she drew in several deep breaths, savoring not just the chill of the air but the scent of it, the clean crispness of it. And she'd come to treasure the privacy of the place, something so far removed from her multistory, always in a crowd life that it still caught her off guard at times. And no one was more surprised than she was at how much she liked it.

A lot of the snow was gone now that the sun had been up a few hours and even up here on the hill the temperature had broken forty degrees, according to the decorative thermometer on the porch. But there was enough

in the shady spots to add a wintry charm to the view,
and she was glad she'd chosen to do this.

They had just reached the edge of the clearing the
cabin sat in when Kyle gently stopped her, whispering to her to look ahead and to the right. "Beside the
Black Hills spruce." She gave him a sideways look. He
grinned at her as he pointed, still speaking quietly. "The
tall, arrowhead-shaped one."

"You did that on purpose." She echoed his quiet tone
even though she didn't know why he was whispering.

"Yep," he admitted, and she had to smother a laugh
as she looked. It took her a moment to spot the tree,
about twenty yards ahead. She didn't see anything there
except the green of the tree, the spots of snow lingering
in its shade, and the brown of the deciduous trees gone
dormant for the winter behind the evergreen.

And then the brown moved. And she found herself
stared at by a pair of dark eyes more intent than any
human eyes she'd ever seen. The antlers atop the animal's head blended into the branches, until he moved.
And she had the strangest feeling that she should freeze
right there and not take another step. "Why do I feel
like the boss just walked in?" she whispered.

His arm came around her, and when she looked up at
him he was grinning. "Good call. Because he is. That's
a bull elk, and you do not want to mess with him. That
guy could take down a bear in a fair fight."

"I believe it. He's big. And those antlers…"

"He'd toss a human a fair distance, I'd guess."

"Only one stupid enough to antagonize him," she
said, feeling more than a little uneasy.

"I saw one with even bigger antlers running through

the trees once," he said. "It's amazing how they do it, and not catch them on something."

She'd never seen an animal this big in the wild before. She'd seen a coyote once, on a road trip, but nothing like this creature in its natural habitat. Clearly she needed to get out of the city more.

Standing arm in arm they watched the majestic animal, and Ashlynn had the thought that here, in this place she'd never expected to be, feeling in a way she'd never thought she would about the man beside her, she was as close to completely happy as she'd ever been. Oh, she'd been content with her life, but she knew now that content and happy were two very different things.

"Oh!" She gave a little start as the elk's head came up sharply. The animal was staring again, but not at them. He was looking downhill. And as if he were seeing something much closer than they were. Then he spun on his hindquarters and took off into the trees. "What—"

Kyle reacted nearly as fast as the elk had, whirling around, looking in the same direction. In the same motion he pushed her behind him and slid the rifle off his shoulder. Ashlynn's heart seemed to jam up into her throat as her pulse took off.

Then she heard a short, harsh laugh, coming from below. And then, a crazily excited male voice.

"Your girl makes a nice target up there, boy. This'll be easy."

The idyll was shattered.

Victor was here.

Chapter 35

Kyle shifted his rifle to a ready position. He mentally prepped himself to shoot if necessary. He had to focus on the fact that the threat they'd come here to avoid was now right in front of them. Somewhere.

His father was many things, including evil, but he'd grown up here and knew his way around in the wilderness. Including how to stay hidden behind the tree line.

He was also, unfortunately, a good shot.

He felt Ash move behind him and reached back with one hand to stop her. "He's armed. Stay behind me."

"But—"

"Ash, please. I have to focus."

He could sense her reluctance, but the plea—and the words he'd chosen because she'd said them herself—apparently did it, because she stopped. He scanned the tree line again, searching for anything out of sync, anything changed from all the times he'd scanned it before.

He had to know where Victor was, so he could be sure he was between him and Ash.

Six rounds. He had six chances to end the threat, assuming his father's first shot didn't succeed. Protecting Ash came first, but he couldn't do that if he was dead. He wished they hadn't come out here, he could defend her in the cabin much better, but it was too late now, and wishing had never gotten him anything or anywhere. If they ran, they'd be easy to pick off. They could try to slowly fall back, but he was fairly certain the moment they moved in that direction Victor would realize the goal and make his move.

It was as he shifted his gaze back toward where the elk had bolted that he saw it. A movement where there shouldn't have been one, just a brief flash of...something, something there and then not, behind the trunk of one of the larger trees. He went with his gut because he had no other choice. He shifted his position slightly, to make sure he was between his father and Ash.

He didn't have much hope he could scare the old man off, but he had to try. It would be worth the expended round if he could convince him to back off. He brought the Winchester to his shoulder, aimed carefully at the tree trunk where he'd seen the movement. Fired.

Ash let out a little scream. The bullet hit the tree, sending bits of bark flying. He saw movement again, this time downward. The old man was ducking. Location confirmed, and message delivered.

"Kyle," she began.

"Just letting him know I know where he is. And that he's not the only one armed."

"Oh. I—"

"Been practicing, kid?"

The yell from the trees was tinged with that same disturbing laugh as before, the censorious laugh Kyle had heard directed at him so many times as a kid.

"Won't do you any good," the harsh, almost maniacal voice came again. "You've still got a lesson to learn about keeping your mouth shut, since it seems the first one didn't take."

Kyle spoke under his breath to Ash. "Let's start working our way back toward the cabin. Just make sure you don't get out from behind me."

"But that makes you a target," she said urgently.

"That's the point," he said flatly. "He wants you dead first, to hurt me as much as possible." At this point he didn't care what he was tacitly admitting to, and the truth of his own words made the next ones sharp. "Move. Slowly."

She was clearly reluctant, and one glance at her showed the fear in her eyes, a fear that jabbed at him like a gutting knife. But she moved.

"She's as good as dead already," his father yelled. "You made sure of that when you fell for her."

Something about the mocking triumph in the man's voice, coupled with that flash of frightened brown eyes, made him snap.

"You'll have to kill me first," he yelled back. "That'll take all the fun out of it for you, you twisted SOB."

"Got that backward, boy. You're the son of a bitch."

"Son of a devil, you mean," he snapped back.

He felt Ash's hand grabbing his arm and only then realized he'd taken a step toward the tree. He turned slightly to her, and one look at the pure emotion in her face stopped him in his tracks.

"No," she whispered. "I can't lose you."

His anger vanished, and all he wanted to do in that moment was kiss her. He wanted time to tell her what she'd come to mean to him, how she had him thinking about changing his entire life around. He wanted to—

He heard the crack of the rifle in almost the same instant that his hat went flying. He pushed her down to the ground, crouching over her protectively, with the rifle aimed down the hill. And then his father stepped out from behind the tree.

He was clad in camo gear, a clear signal he was on an intentional hunt. As if the rifle at his shoulder wasn't enough to signal that. Even from here Kyle could see that grin on the man's face, the one that usually preceded some act of cruelty or brutality.

He brought the Winchester back up to his shoulder. Sighted in. Slid his finger to the trigger.

It would be a mercy to the world. To end that malevolent life. To end the man who had just shot at him. The man who wanted Ash dead, just to hurt his own son.

He tightened his finger. Felt the trigger start to give. Hesitated. His own father? Had it come to that?

Another shot. He felt a tug at his shoulder, but oddly no pain. Ash had been out of the path, that was all that mattered. Again he tried to make his finger move that last fraction of an inch.

His father turned slightly, looking toward the downhill side. The instant he moved there was another shot. This time not from his father. From farther down the hill. Louder, a larger gauge. A split second later his father went to his knees. Kyle watched, stunned as the man tried even now to raise the rifle toward them. But he crumpled completely a moment later.

Kyle stared, not sure what had happened.

"What…you didn't fire, so who did?" Ash asked, scrambling back up onto her knees.

"I don't know."

His gaze was fixed on the unmoving figure of his father. Disbelief was churning in him. It couldn't be. Could it be? Could it be over? Really, truly over? He stood up, slowly, half expecting it to be a feint, that the old man would roll over and come up shooting.

He didn't.

"Stay here," he said to Ash. To his relief she didn't argue, although she once more didn't look happy about it.

He started toward the collapsed figure. Slowly, rifle at the ready. Watching for any movement, any sign that there was still breath left in that very still body.

There was nothing.

When he reached it—for that's what his father was now—he saw why. That shot from down the hill had hit him in the chest, and he'd gone down fast. He—

The sound of a motor from down the hill cut through his thoughts. He spun that way, wondering what new threat this could be. For a moment he just stared blankly as the marked sheriff's car pulled into view. What was he doing here? How had he known? The tall, lean man in uniform got out, settling his hat on his head as he started toward them. Kyle recognized not a deputy but the sheriff himself, Frank Noonan.

"I didn't shoot him," he said almost urgently as the man knelt beside what was clearly now a body, checking for a pulse anyway.

Noonan straightened up, and looked at Kyle with a steady, cool pair of blue eyes. "I know. I did. Better me than you having to shoot your own father."

Kyle nearly gaped at him; he never would have expected the man to even think about that. As if he'd somehow known, even from…wherever he'd been down the hill, that Kyle wouldn't be able to pull that trigger on his father. Kyle wondered what kind of rifle sat in the marked unit. Something with a purpose-designed scope, he guessed. He was more than grateful for it, and for this man who obviously knew how to use it.

"You two all right?" Noonan asked.

"Yes. Thanks to you."

"And his lousy shooting," Ash said rather grimly, and he saw that she was holding his now-ventilated cowboy hat. She also reached up to finger the hole in the sleeve of his jacket, and he realized just how lucky he'd gotten.

The man in uniform touched the brim of his own hat as he nodded at Ash. "Frank Noonan," he said by way of introduction.

"Sorry," Kyle said hastily. "This is Ashlynn Colton."

She smiled at the man, who nodded and smiled back. "Sorry it took me so long, but I was some distance away."

"Perfect timing, seems to me," Ashlynn said.

"I was afraid I'd be too late."

"How did you know…he was here?" she asked.

Kyle hadn't even thought to wonder that yet. He guessed he was more in shock than he'd realized.

"Got a call from Elliott this morning," Noonan answered. "He spotted someone headed this way, knew you were up here and had pretty much guessed why."

"I…didn't know he knew anything about it," Kyle said.

"Said he'd noticed you'd been spooked lately, then you vanished, and that it probably had something to do with that guy hanging around he'd seen you talking to.

Because you'd been about the color of that snow over there afterward. Then you disappeared, so he put two and two together. He's a sharp guy."

"Yeah. Yeah, he is. I owe him."

"Be sure you let him know, when we get back to the ranch."

Kyle nodded, although his mind was tumbling. If Elliott had called this morning, then Victor could have been here for hours. Watching. Waiting. And it hit him like a sucker punch that he'd waited, not making any move that would betray his presence until what he'd been waiting for had happened.

Ash had come outside.

He fought down a shudder. Glanced at the body of the man who'd both given him life and made that life hell.

"Don't feel bad about this," Noonan said quietly.

"I…don't. Even after you shot him, he spent the last three seconds of his life still trying to hurt me by killing Ash."

"Some people are just messed up," Noonan said. "But it's over now."

Kyle felt a wave of exhaustion sweep over him. He'd never felt anything like it before, this kind of enervating fog that seemed to envelop him. If he was asked later—Noonan had mentioned something about an official enquiry that would wrap up quickly—he wasn't sure he would even be able to explain it all.

Right now, he wasn't sure of anything except that he couldn't seem to think at all. It was crazy; his father had barely been part of his life for years, yet now he looked at him lying there, the rifle he'd meant to kill Ash with beside him, and he felt as if his entire life had been as exploded as the man's cold heart had been by a well-placed bullet.

He didn't know what to feel or how to feel it. Maybe he was just numb. So he simply followed Noonan's directions, glad the man was there to take charge. He half listened as the next steps were explained, wondered vaguely if he'd be able to make sense at all when it came time to make what Noonan called his statement.

And when he very belatedly realized that when Noonan said it was over now, it also applied to the reason he'd had the best few days of his life, here in this isolated place with Ashlynn.

Chapter 36

Ashlynn sat alone, back in her cabin, trying not to panic.

It was Monday morning and she hadn't seen Kyle since she'd given her own statement and a deputy had brought her back to the ranch. He had likely spent the weekend tied up with all the paperwork and details—and how well did she know how long that kind of thing took, especially when it involved a death?—and she had no idea if he was back home, or what state he was in.

He'd clearly been rattled, almost a wreck, when the high tension of the last couple of weeks had so abruptly ended. Ended with the death of the man who had so malevolently shaped his life. Who had set him on that course of always moving on, never settling in one place.

Would that change now? Would Kyle be able to change the pattern of a lifetime, that of ever and always moving on? And doing it ever and always alone? That he no longer had to might not be enough to break that long-standing habit. Because nothing could ever change what had set him on that path, the murder of the woman he'd loved.

She'd tried not to do it, but in the end had caved, at about 2:00 a.m. that first night alone, when she was lying there still sleepless. Missing him, his warmth, the feel of him, the simple knowledge that he was there beside her, that she could reach for him and he would respond. She'd finally gotten up and gone to her usual place, her laptop.

She'd dug back and found the news reports on the death of Sarah Seaver. And the trial afterward, where Kyle had testified his father had plotted it and bragged about what he was going to do ahead of time, down to the detail of shoving her in front of a speeding truck.

She knew which one to believe now.

One of the articles included a photo of the victim. She'd found herself looking at an open, honest face, with wide, clear blue eyes and pale blond hair pulled back into a sleek ponytail.

Only the determined set of her jaw gave a clue to the strength she had had. She remembered what Kyle had told her about how she'd stood up to Victor, for his sake. How she'd never backed down, with that strength that had, in the end, gotten her killed.

She'd stared at the image for a long time, until she'd degenerated into comparing herself to the other woman, wondering if she would have had the courage to stand up for Kyle the way this woman had. She wanted to think she would have.

She knew she would now. The man had shown himself willing to lay his life down to protect her, and while she knew there were many reasons for that—such as who he was at the core—she also knew one of them was that he cared for her.

Loved her?

That she didn't know. She only knew she loved him.

She understood that he was an emotional wreck just now, although he likely wouldn't admit it. Still he needed some time on his own to work through everything that had happened. And so here she was, sitting in her guest cabin, wondering if Kyle was going to turn up soon and tell her he was moving on, as he always did. That their interlude in the isolated cabin had been just that and only that. How could their lives possibly mix the way she wanted them to? It wasn't simply the geographical distance between them, it was the old cliché, city girl, country boy. How could they ever combine the two? Sure, a lot of her work could be done remotely, if she had access…

And idea flickered in the back of her mind. A possibility. But before she could begin her usual analysis, the team phone chimed a notification. She pulled up the app to find a text from her CSI expert brother, Patrick. A long one. And the more she read, the more her heart began to pound.

Asked prime suspect to meet with me to go over one of my reports from the second crime scene. Looking for reaction. Got one: not just a no show at the meeting, but at work at all. Checked his place, no sign of him, and warranted search looks like he packed up the essentials in a hurry. Seems he's done a runner.

As of now, other suspects are back-burnered. Focus on #1.

Ashlynn acknowledged the text, but then sat for a long moment, staring at the screen. It was true. It was really true; she was certain of it now. Xander was the Landmark Killer. They didn't have enough evidence yet to put him away, she knew that, but there was no doubt in her own mind.

A second text came in, this one from her brother Brennan.

Nice work, Ashlynn. You found the key on this one.

Ditto that. That one was from Patrick.

We could have done without you getting on another killer's radar, though.

She stared at the line sent by Cash. She hadn't said anything about Victor, how could they have—

You didn't really think we'd let our baby sister trek off to the wilds of Montana and not keep track of what was going on, did you?

She could almost hear Cash's teasing, big brother tone in that text. And the part of her that wanted to be miffed that they were checking up on her was smothered quickly by the part of her that loved her brothers and was grateful that they loved her enough to worry about her. It was part of being a Colton, that that bond, those family ties, were strong, tight and never wavered.

And it struck her that this was something she sometimes took for granted that Kyle had never, ever known. And suddenly she wanted very much to make that happen. She wanted him to know that her family would stand by him as his own had not. And they would, given he'd risked his own life to protect her. Given he'd nearly taken a bullet for her.

But for that to happen, some changes were going to have to happen.

Yeah, yeah, she texted back, but at the risk of being unprofessional she added a heart. Then she quickly went back to business. I'll alert the sheriff here, but I don't think the suspect will come back.

Agreed, came Patrick's response. Confirm with your contact there, but from what you've said he hated that place and himself when he lived there. I think he'll stay here in the city. He feels powerful here, and unfindable.

She sent back a quick acknowledgement, and when they had all signed off she was back to sitting alone in silence.

Confirm with your contact…

Your contact. As if that was all he was to her. Of course, as far as her brothers knew, that's all Kyle was. Boy, did they have a surprise coming. At least, she hoped they did. She hoped beyond hope that Kyle wasn't even now planning his next move to a new job in a new place. Maybe it had become a habit he couldn't break, even with the reason for it now gone for good.

She dug out the card the sheriff had given her with his direct number handwritten on it. In her gratitude that the man had saved Kyle from a horrible decision, that of killing his own father, she'd lightly teased him about sharing that number with a fed. Noonan had given her a smile and said, "I won't hold it against you."

With that kind smile in mind she called the number.

And somewhat to her surprise, after four rings the man himself really did answer. Things were definitely different here; getting to the top guy back home would have probably taken a couple of hours. Days, if you were a stranger to him, as she essentially was to Noonan.

She quickly gave him an update on the case, alerting him both that Xander was now suspect number one, and also that this was "a just in case" call, that the consensus was Xander would be staying in the city. She offered to send up updated info and photos, but Noonan declined both.

"I ran across him a few times as a deputy," he said, rather sourly. "I'll recognize him, even in city duds."

She hesitated, then plunged ahead, figuring she'd never have a better segue. "Did you run across Kyle, too?"

"Before now, just once, during his father's trial." The man paused, then said, "He did the right thing when it couldn't have been easy. He's a good man. A man you can trust."

"Yes. Yes, he is."

"Hope he got some rest yesterday. He looked pretty rough when he left here."

She wasn't even sure what she said to that, and felt silly for not wanting to admit she hadn't seen him. Had he even come back here, to the ranch? Or had he come back just long enough to grab his stuff and move on? Without even telling her, let alone doing it face-to-face?

The moment she thought it, that one phrase Noonan had said ran through her mind again and again.

A man you could trust.

She wondered why he'd felt compelled to tell her that.

Was she wearing some kind of sign on her forehead?
Hey, I'm crazy about this guy!

She laughed ruefully at herself.

Then she was on her feet, pacing yet again. She was used to being able to focus completely on the task at hand. Problem was, right now she had too many tasks at hand. And for the first time since she'd joined her brothers at the FBI, one of those tasks outranked them.

Maybe she should go over to Kyle's cabin. After all, she did have reason to see him, to give him an update, if only because they'd all agreed his half brother wasn't likely to show up here. That bit of peace was worth delivering, wasn't it? Or was she just looking for an excuse?

You need to give him space. He's had an awful lot to process, and it will take time.

Besides, what would she do if he wasn't there?

This kind of mental merry-go-round was exhausting. And she hated being indecisive. She searched for something, anything, that screamed out "Yes, this is what you need to do."

And finally it struck her to go find Elliott. She needed to thank him, didn't she, for sending Sheriff Noonan after them? And while doing that, surely he'd mention if he'd seen Kyle? Two birds, she thought.

She spun around, crossed to the dresser to grab up the jacket she'd tossed there, and headed for the door.

Chapter 37

Kyle marveled a little at the horse's patience. Splash wasn't known for it, but he was exhibiting it now, as this human brushed him endlessly. Kyle knew he was doing it because he needed the distraction. Because he had so much to think about, he didn't even know where to start.

"I gotta say, Slater, you've got a knack." Matt's voice came from where his boss leaned against the bottom half of the stall door.

"Thanks," he said. Then he patted the young Appy's neck. "He's a good horse."

"He behaves for you, and for kids, but nobody else," the man said dryly.

And Ash. He was good for Ash. "He's got spirit," he said carefully.

"A little too much, for our purposes. With that new project coming up, and the cost, Dad's looking to cut back on the horses guests can't ride."

Kyle's head snapped around sharply. Surely he wouldn't geld him—James Wesley was a horseman, and he had to have seen the breeding potential in the colt. So he went with the more likely option, the one Kyle had feared all along. "He's going to sell him?"

Damn, he'd miss the colt. A lot. Where would he be going? Maybe that could be his next job. Even as he thought it he quashed the thought. One of those things he was avoiding thinking about, and had been since the nightmare with Victor had finally ended.

"Not exactly," Matt said. "He's decided to use him to pay off a debt."

Kyle's brow furrowed. "A debt?"

"To someone the silly horse already likes. Someone who did him a solid that resulted in a certain Mr. Fisher going to bat for the ranch in that permit inquiry last week."

He'd forgotten, amid the chaos, about the questions that would determine whether or not that new bunkhouse, designed especially for sick kids, got built, but he recognized the name right away.

"Dylan," he said, remembering the withdrawn, heartbroken little boy. They were giving the colt to the kid? He was a bit too young, but his parents could certainly afford someone to take care of the horse. But they lived in town, they wouldn't have—

"So, sometime today head up to the big house. There's some paperwork."

Kyle blinked. "What?"

"Transfer of ownership, all that hassle you get with a registered animal."

Belatedly Kyle got there. "He's giving him…to me? That's crazy, he's worth way too much."

Matt smiled widely then. "I think somewhere in there is the hope you'll stay, but we also know things have changed for you, in a big way." A twinkle came into his boss's eyes. "And I don't mean getting out from under that rotten excuse for a father you had." Matt turned as if to go, then looked back. "Good luck, Kyle. Whatever your path. And now you have company."

He stared at his boss's back as he walked away, and was beyond grateful that he'd landed here, at this time, when he'd needed it most. But then all other thoughts vanished from his mind.

...you have company.

Did he mean he had company here and now or...on that path he mentioned? He tried to quash the images that raced through his mind then, of a future, somewhere, anywhere, of being happy as long as Ash was with him. Then he heard footsteps and knew Matt had meant company here and now.

And it was Ash.

He didn't need to lean out of the stall to know it was her. Splash told him. The little Appy walked eagerly to the door and popped his head over the top, nickering softly.

And then she was there, patting the young horse with confidence now. Her eyes looked a little tired, as if she hadn't slept any more than he had. But now that he saw her, he regretted that he hadn't made the effort when he'd first gotten back to the ranch, after that seemingly endless time spent with Sheriff Noonan and detectives, giving his statement and being questioned endlessly.

But since, as the sheriff pointed out, he had to justify taking lethal action, Kyle had felt compelled to do everything he could to make sure it was clear there had been no other choice. And wondered anew at the kind of man who would take on such a load, to save him from having to shoot his own father. That there weren't enough of them in this world was the only thing he'd been certain of when he'd finally been told he could go.

And when he'd gotten back to the ranch, somehow facing Ashlynn seemed…impossible. Probably because the threat here was over now, as was their time alone together. And the bitter irony of it stabbed at him, that the time he'd spent with her in that high country cabin, trying to dodge a killer, had become as close to paradise as he would ever likely come.

"Elliott told me you were in here," she said quietly, the first words she'd spoken except for some murmuring to Splash. "I found him outside, to thank him."

"I thanked him, too," he said, relieved at the relatively ordinary topic. "If he hadn't called Sheriff Noonan…"

"Yes." She wasn't looking at Kyle, but still rubbing at the delighted colt's nose. Which made Kyle remember the many ways she'd touched him, during those nights—and a couple of afternoons as well—at the high country cabin.

At last, with a final pat for Splash, she looked up and met his gaze. There was a long moment of silence, spinning out until he was scrambling for something, anything, to say other than what was boiling up inside him, a desperate hope that although the threat was over, they weren't.

"I got some info from my team this morning."

That slapped him right back into reality. "I—you did?"

She nodded. "My brother Patrick agrees with your assessment that Xander wouldn't come back here. That he'll stay in New York where he feels confident, powerful."

"Not to mention being the target-rich environment," he said, his tone dry. He was surprised he was able to talk about it so...unemotionally. Except for a little jab of...something, that her brother the FBI agent agreed with him.

"That, too," she said. "He's on his course now, and Sinead doesn't think he'll swerve off of it."

"She's the profiler?" When she nodded his mouth quirked. "Interesting family dynamic you've got there."

She smiled at that. "Yes. It took some convincing, since it's hardly policy to put family members on the same team, but once they let us try, we compiled a success rate they can't argue with."

"Glad to hear there's that much sense left there."

She smiled wryly. And changed the subject. "Did I hear correctly? Mr. Wesley is giving you Splash?"

He couldn't help smiling back as he gave a wondering shake of his head. "It seems that way." He leaned over and gave the colt a solid slap on the neck, to which Splash snorted happily in response. He explained the reasoning behind the gift.

"That review they posted was what led me here," she said.

And there it was. Right in front of him. Unavoidable. And because he didn't know what else to do, he went with the first thing that popped into his mind.

"Then I owe them three times over."

She blinked. "Three times?"

"That's what got me the foreman's old place, now Splash...and brought you here."

She just looked at him for a long moment, and then

her expression shifted as she said, "They're good people here, the Wesleys, and Elliott, all of them."

"Yes," he said, wondering why she looked suddenly almost sad. "They are. And they've been really good to me."

"Do you feel as if you owe them? Like you…should stay, I mean?"

He blinked. Was she talking about his habit of moving on every year, or something else? Something more? Something…between them?

…*things have changed for you, in a big way.* Matt's words came back to him suddenly. Had everyone guessed that something unexpected had happened in their time up on the hill? And did they believe it was something that could be permanent? Did *he* believe it could be permanent? Did she?

"Why are you asking?" He barely managed to get the words out.

"Isn't it obvious?" she said softly.

"This," he said carefully, "is not something I want to guess at."

She smiled at that. "It is kind of important for guesswork, isn't it? So I guess I'll just flat out ask. Do you want—"

And then, at the worst possible moment, he heard the now familiar buzz of her cell phone signaling a message coming in. This was why he hated the damned things; their timing so often sucked.

"Sorry, it's the team phone, I have to—"

"I know. Do it."

She pulled it out and a moment later was staring at the screen. She read the message quickly, and her expression changed just as fast, going from intense to concern to…anger? He wouldn't have been sure of the last if he hadn't heard her mutter "You bastard," under her breath.

"Literally or figuratively?" he asked when after a moment she hadn't spoken again.

She looked up at him then, and he saw a fierce gleam in her eyes. And suddenly he realized that she wasn't just someone who knew her way around computers and how to use them to find just about anything, she was a full, determined and dedicated member of this team.

"Both," she said flatly.

He knew then that she was talking about Xander. Had he killed again? While they were trying to avoid being killed by his father, had someone else been killed by his half brother?

And suddenly it all seemed impossible, all the hopes he'd foolishly allowed himself, about some kind of future for them. Because why would she want anything to do with a guy with a killer father and brother?

Ashlynn Colton was much too smart for that.

Chapter 38

Ashlynn had to tamp down her anger as she read the text message from her brother again.

Another text from our suspect. He's aiming at me now, so I think Ashlynn leaving the city worked. Forwarding here:

Remember how you missed collecting DNA evidence a few years ago from that Upper East Side hotel and the killer struck again because of you? Sort of like now. You'll never get me.

A second text came in. Short, to the point, and determined.

We will.

Yes, they would. She had no doubt of that, because she had faith in them all. They were relentless when it came to their work. And now that they were nearly certain it was a traitor from within, they would be ruthless.

But she also knew Xander's words—because she was utterly certain now it was him—got to Patrick. He'd been furious after the DNA incident the text mentioned, and it had taken him a while to calm down about it. What had happened hadn't been his fault, not directly, but he'd been the lead CSI on that case and therefore held himself responsible. Because that's who her brother was.

"Did he kill again?"

She looked up from the screen. Kyle's expression was utterly bleak. She hated seeing him look that way, hated the pain he must be feeling. Even though he and Xander had never been close, never really been brothers, it would be impossible not to feel…something about all this.

"No," she hastened to assure him. "He's sniping, at us. My brother Patrick, specifically."

A third text came in, drawing her attention back to the screen. This one was from Sinead.

Ashlynn, he's not focused on you any longer. And he doesn't move backward. I think you can come home.

Home. Come home.

She lifted her gaze to Kyle. "Sinead says I can come home."

He went very still. He looked about to speak, but then turned his head, focusing on Splash, who had been getting restless. He went back to brushing the colt as if the simple task required his full concentration.

"Kyle—"

"So when will you be leaving?"

His voice was so expressionless it gave her a chill. And she had the sudden feeling that her answer to this could be crucial. She called up everything she knew, everything she'd ever learned from witnessing the twins' interrogations over the years. Added in what she knew of this man. And then there was the prime element, the simple fact that she loved him and did not want to try to live without him in her life.

It took her a moment to be able to speak. "I was about to ask you the same thing."

His head came up then. "What?"

"It's almost time for you to move on, right? You've been here for six months."

"I..."

"But how will you take Splash with you? Do you have a trailer?"

"I...no."

"Then will you stay here? Was that the trade for giving you Splash?"

His brow furrowed. He was thinking, at least. "No, Matt said—"

"Are you happy to be all over the local news again, because of your father?"

"No!"

And now she'd hit his gut feeling. So she went with the thought that had occurred to her during those sleepless hours.

"Ever heard of the Hudson River Valley?"

He blinked. "Hudson…as in the New York City Hudson?"

She nodded, smiling. "It's so much more than just that. It's over three hundred miles long, and it starts a long way away from the city. Up in the Adirondack Mountains."

He was looking at her steadily now, as if he'd decided to just be patient with her, as he was with Splash, and this line of questioning that as yet made no sense to him.

"You mean those hills they call mountains back east?" he asked, in the tonal equivalent of an eye roll.

"Well, I admit, they're not the Rockies," she said, a smile tugging at the corners of her mouth.

"Every mountain in the Rockies is three times taller than the tallest one of those," he countered.

There you go. She said it mentally to some of the people she knew back in the city. *Don't ever think he's some ignorant country rube, because he's not. He reads, and he remembers.*

She realized she was thinking as if she'd already convinced him, and made herself slow down.

"Still, they are mountains."

"Only because nobody can agree when a hill becomes a mountain."

"Point taken," she agreed, letting the smile loose this time as her heart gave a little leap at the thought of spending endless hours having conversations like this with him. She took in a deep breath and made the plunge. "But the river is a river, and the Hudson River Valley is beautiful. Lots of orchards and farms. Places that could easily handle horses. It would be different in scope, but the same kind of life you have here. We could find one that would be a good place for Splash to grow up. I could commute, and I sure wouldn't miss my little fifth-floor walkup."

He was staring at her, all trace of neutrality—and teasing—vanished now. She let the silence spin out because she didn't know what to say that wouldn't sound like begging. *Come with me, Kyle. Please, I don't want to be without you.*

"That kind of life would be way too quiet for you," he said after a moment.

"I thought so too, once. But here…here I learned that I really do love the open spaces. That it's wonderful to have a quiet place to decompress." *If I have someone I love to do it with.*

"What," he finally said, very carefully, "are you asking me?"

Okay, maybe she would have to spell it out. Have to beg. And she realized with a little jolt that for him, she would. But then something else hit her, something that might be a deciding factor.

"Don't you think you might be happier where no one has ever heard of your father?"

"Ashlynn Colton, are you asking me to go with you?" Something new had come into his voice, something that she very much wanted to hear as hope. She'd be hideously embarrassed if she was wrong…

So what? You're leaving anyway, you have to get back home, to work, back to the team. Do you really want to do that without taking your best shot at the only thing you've ever wanted just as much?

"Yes," she said simply. "I am." Splash nickered, pushing at her with his nose. "Yes, you too," she assured the animal, patting him. "You could be the start of a string of Appaloosas in New York."

Kyle let out a long, audible breath and his eyes closed for a moment. She went on quietly.

"You'd have to be kind of low profile until we catch Xander, but we're getting close. And I know you love this place, this life. But I have to be there, within reach of the city. We could come back for vacations, here to the ranch." He opened his eyes again and she smiled at him. "Assuming you could take a break from your prosperous horse breeding venture, of course."

"You're...sure about this?"

"I am." She kept her gaze fastened on him and brought out her final weapon putting everything she was feeling into it. "I love you, Kyle. I know it's crazy, too fast, and all of that. But it's still true. Come with me."

There was a brief silence as something new and different came into his eyes. And then, quietly but with certainty, he said, "All right."

Joy burst to life in her. She only now admitted to herself how afraid she'd been that he'd say no. That she'd foolishly overwhelmed him, that she was crazy for even thinking he might leave this place, this life.

Kyle turned to Splash and patted the colt's neck. "What do you say, boy? You up to a two-thousand-mile road trip?"

She hadn't really thought about that, actually getting the horse there, but he clearly had, and that quickly. Another reminder to never underestimate that agile brain. In fact, she could think of a few people in the city she'd like to prank, luring them in with his casual demeanor and maybe the hat, and then watch as he applied his own brand of logic and brainpower and took them down a notch. Or two.

Splash nickered again in response, this time nudging

Kyle's hand. As he rubbed the horse's nose he turned his head to look at her.

"By the way, I love you, too."

She felt color flood her cheeks. She hadn't expected that, even after her own admission, not this soon. But then she realized she should have known, because why else would he pack up his entire life and move it two-thirds of the way across the country simply because she asked?

He took one long step, and then he was kissing her. She felt the bottom half of the stall door digging into her but she didn't care. She didn't care about anything other than he was kissing her, and that he'd said yes. She was going back, but life would never be the same. She couldn't wait to introduce him to her brothers. They would rag on him, jab at him, test him—she knew they would. But she also knew they'd never really get to the man who had already withstood so much in his life. And once they knew his strength, his steadfastness, they would accept him completely, because that's who they were.

Life would be what she'd always wanted it to be, but never hoped would really happen.

She couldn't wait.

* * * * *

#2255 CSI COLTON AND THE WITNESS
The Coltons of New York • by Linda O. Johnston

When Patrick Colton's fellow CSI investigator Kyra Patel sees a murderer fleeing a scene, he vows to keep the expectant single mom out of the line of fire. But will the culprit be captured before their growing unprofessional feelings tempt them both?

#2256 OPERATION TAKEDOWN
Cutter's Code • by Justine Davis

As a former soldier, Jordan Crockett knows the truth about his best friend's military death. But convincing Emily Bishop, his deceased buddy's sister, exposes them both to a dangerous web of family secrets...and those determined to keep Jordan silenced.

#2257 HOTSHOT HERO FOR THE HOLIDAYS
Hotshot Heroes • by Lisa Childs

Firefighter Trent Miles *stops* fires—not starts them. But when his house burns down and a body is found inside, he becomes Detective Heather Bolton's number one murder suspect. Their undercover dating ruse to flush out the killer may save Trent from jail, but will Heather's heart be collateral damage?

#2258 OLLERO CREEK CONSPIRACY
Fuego, New Mexico • by Amber Leigh Williams

Luella Decker wants to leave her heartbreaking past behind her. Including her secret romance with rancher Ellis Eaton. But when the animals at her home are targeted and a long-buried family cover-up comes to light, Ellis may be the only one she can trust to keep her alive.

HARLEQUIN
PLUS

Try the best multimedia
subscription service for romance
readers like you!

Read, Watch and Play.

Experience the easiest way to get
the romance content you crave.

Start your **FREE TRIAL** at
<u>www.harlequinplus.com/freetrial</u>.